TWO DEAD DISSIDENTS

James Meakin

CONTENTS

To all those who read my drafts and provided me with a myriad of ideas. Matthew Bland, for tirelessly reading several drafts. James Colombo, who really brought many of the settings alive by pointing out that I had originally forgotten to mention any smells. Oliver Shaw, who convinced me to take this project further. My Mum, Sheila, for being a better editor than any other, and my Dad, Mike, who provided constant ironclad support throughout the creation process despite his tepidity towards reading!

PREFACE

I have been fascinated by murder mysteries from an early age. My Mum lent me several short stories of Agatha Christie's Poirot. I watched the adaptations on *ITV* starring David Suchet. As the years went by, I gradually found came to found out why - it is the duel of wits between reader and writer. Can you guess the murderer, method and motive before the detective does? The writer deliberately impedes your task by throwing in red-herrings making you think you are certain to have guessed the outcome to the letter - until the author puts your thought process to shame in the closing scenes.

Key to any murder mystery is entertainment - be that through settings, characters or dialogue. Failing to solve a puzzle is often an intellectually unpleasant task. With a cryptic crossword, the setting is you, a pencil and a piece of paper. In this book, as was the case in the 'golden age' of crime fiction, you will be transported to opulent settings, experience unusual characters and occasionally witty dialogue. The puzzle will be an escapist and enjoyable one, alongside being an intellectual challenge for the reader.

The entertainment aspect matters for another very important reason. Our current time is grim. We have been through months of isolation, sickness, death, economic hardship and boredom. *Two Dead Dissidents* attempts to be an antithesis to 2020 and much of 2021. The crime novelists of the inter-war period took a similar approach in a time of war, pandemics, economic crisis and political instability. Poirot and Miss Marple solved cases in

English country houses, planes and (most famously) the Orient Express. Readers would be provided with an insight into the lives of racing drivers, explorers, nobles and politicians. The allusion to Art Deco style settings and the train throughout *Two Dead Dissidents* is a memento to this 'golden age' of crime writing. As was the case in the inter-war period, what I aim to do is to capture a point of light and adventurism in an era of darkness and doldrums.

My book is set across many unusual locations across Europe - such Brest and Minsk in Belarus. Even though many novels have been partially set in Paris and Moscow, the fact that few people will have been to said cities recently means that simply flaneuring on paper is an exotic act. Taking in the 'feeling' of foreign countries will hopefully transport the reader back to the (viewed from today's perspective) halcyon days of 2019.

Critics may lambast said approach as a BTEC attempt at Boy's Own/Sir Walter Scott/Alexandre Dumas/Jules Verne. Christie herself was accused of creating one-dimensional characters. A castigation of the following pages for being 'fantastical,' 'romantic,' or 'not dealing with real-life issues and people' would not only be tautology but a vindication of my writing. That is not to say this book totally ignores the social and political context such as COVID-19, debates over policing and the geopolitical situation in Eastern Europe. A discussion of politics, society and culture in the 2020s is secondary to the enjoyment and intellectual challenge of solving the mystery that awaits.

James Meakin

CHAPTER 1: TWO DEAD DISSIDENTS

8th October 2023.

In the Metropolitan Police's Counter-Terrorism Unit, DCI Len Tidworth was having a tough morning. The DCI was sitting in his private office on an office chair made out of leather from a country club. He was sweating and jaded at his file-covered desk sitting in his suit and tie whilst drinking a cup of coffee. It was only 8:30 am and two prominent Russian dissidents from the Yasnaya Polyana Theatre Group had been murdered overnight on an East London industrial estate. Tidworth had worked on the Skripal case five years earlier. On the TV monitor inside his office, he was watching *Good Morning Britain*. Piers Morgan was presenting the programme. It was Piers's first appearance back after his two-and-a-half-year hiatus from *ITV*. He was livid at the murders and the British government. In fact, it was difficult to tell whether he was angrier at Vladimir Putin or Boris Johnson.

With clenched fists, a massive grimace and blushing cheeks, he launched into his diatribe about the murders.

"This is a disgrace," he said, almost spitting his words rather than speaking them, "An absolute bloody disgrace."

"I don't think it is necessary to use such language," interrupted his co-host, Susanna Reid, with some desperation, "it is not even 9 *am* let alone 9 pm."

"I am not going to be told exactly what words to use when the British government has clearly failed to protect people fleeing

from a heinous regime. It has failed time and time again when people need it most," he thundered whilst banging the desk. "Actually, you know what," with his mood changing from angry to fatalistic exasperation whilst pointing his finger at the camera like a pistol, "If our government is going to be so weak with the Russians, I don't blame them for acting like this!"
Tidworth abruptly switched off the TV and muttered in disgust, "Piers, oh dear. What a pillock."

Since Tidworth was investigating a murder with international and diplomatic ramifications for Anglo-Russian relations, not to mention one that would certainly capture the public imagination, he would need help from the Army Intelligence Corps to find the culprits. Captain Daniel Holloway from the Intelligence Corps walked into Tidworth's private office for a one-on-one just before 9 am. Holloway was a heavily built man in his mid to late twenties yet was only about five foot eight, so he had the stature of an avid gym user. In fact, he had played hockey at public school and had just come back from a morning gym session, so he smelt of that typical musty, fragrant and pungent male sports shower gel – probably Nivea or L'Oreal. Holloway conducted himself with the typical confidence and smattering of arrogance, of a British Army officer. His gait was very much like a march – almost to the point that it felt like all that marching on the parade ground had imprinted itself on him. Though he was wearing mufti, a tight fitting dark grey suit and tie, the gait was a giveaway for Tidworth's colleagues that he was military. His manner when speaking was stiff, bland and pompous. He was clearly intelligent, analytical and knowledgeable, but he would stand up straight with his hands on his hips, with few gesticulations. Tidworth on the other hand, possessed a bit of a camp sheriff's swagger - he had obviously been watching too many westerns when he was younger. Nonetheless, Tidworth and Holloway did possess something in common. The former had served in the Parachute Regiment for about 15 years before joining the police force – and it was obvious to anyone entering Tidworth's den that he had been in the military. There were trinkets from the Middle East and the Balkans, a red beret and several metal sports trophies, including a regimental boxing tournament that he had won in 1999. The room was quite dark so, aided by the various paraphernalia and the leather chair, it unfortunately gave off the impression of a cluttered pensioner's living room.

Tidworth grasped Holloway's hand tightly and they sat down.
"Good to have a military man on the case. Well, as you are Intel Corps, kind of military," said Tidworth in his Mancunian accent with grinning glee at the joke he had just made about the Intelligence Corps' low ranking on the British Army's Order of Precedence. Holloway was also waiting for the inevitable jab about being a 'Rupert.'
"So, I presume you are ex-military. Oh, and by the way do you have some hand gel?" enquired Holloway in contrasting received pronunciation, not at all fazed by Tidworth's predictable jab at his Corps.
Tidworth passed the hand gel over to Holloway who put a dollop on his hand.
"Yeah, Paras. I was in 2 PARA and I did two tours of Northern Ireland in the 1990s, along with a stint in Bosnia before my tours of Iraq and Afghanistan. I left in 2005 and the police made sense for me. You know, these Russkies are getting more and more tetchy and frisky but you could never top the IRA in their day. Do you remember that lad who used to kill informants with a slab?"
"I do."
"Russian Spetsnatz could parachute into Londonderry, say 'Londonderry' here not 'Derry,' and I bet you that by end of the day they would all be turned into sausages! Anyway, there will probably be a bit of aggro between London and Moscow, Piers Morgan will have an explosion on Breakfast TV and some diplomats will go home and rinse and repeat! I know the drill."

Holloway was perturbed that Tidworth had not asked him any

questions about his military service Instead, the ex-Para rather incoherently rambled on about his thoughts on the IRA, the murder case and Piers Morgan. Tidworth's aloofness and dismissive nature towards Holloway gave him the impression that Tidworth believed he was a pen-pusher in contrast to the ex-Special Forces soldier with years of experience in the field.

Holloway and Tidworth then went into a larger meeting room with Tidworth's other colleagues DS Ravi Chakravarty and DC Jo Hardy. Holloway was introduced to them, bumping elbows with each. Holloway sat on his own on one side of the table and Chakravarty and Hardy sat on the other side. Tidworth was supposed to be sitting at the head of the table, but he decided to stand up next to a whiteboard at one end of the room. He was like a big cat surveying his realm. The pictures of his possible prey were about to be pinned to the whiteboard.

"Right!" he said with the emphasis of a Shakespearean actor and the grunt of a pig, "let's have a look at this group of thesps. The victims were a 38-year old writer called Yev-uhh-gen-uhh-ia Tik-uhh-on-uhh-ova? Any smart arses here like to give me some help. Ravi? Anyone?"
"Yevgeniya Tikhonova," replied Holloway who, if Tidworth had been bothered to ask, was fluent in Russian.
"My my, you're not one of *them* are you?" asked Tidworth with an inquisitive look on his face.
"No of course not. I had to learn it to be an Intel Analyst."
"So, Rupert, I suppose you could help me with the next one."
"Alexey Ostrovsky." Holloway let out a big huff. Aside from the policeman's lame attempts at class-based military humour, he was more frustrated with Tidworth's general incompetent obfuscation
"Right! This lad was also 40 and he was one of the actors. They both escaped from Russia in 2012 and have lived together since. They were last seen leaving their house in Islington at about 1:35 am. It seems as if they travelled to Shadwell and this in-

dustrial estate and they died there with gunshots in the back of their head."

"Seems like an execution. Russian special services style. Like the Katyn Massacre in Poland. 10,000 people all shot with a bullet in the back of the head at close range. This murder seems highly suspicious and if Russian Intel is involved, we need to get on top of this quickly. Who else do they associate themselves with?"

"Our Ravi will show you who."

DS Chakravarty put pictures of potential suspects on the whiteboard.

"We first have the lead actor and director of their next play "the Cranes are Dying." His name is Edmund Drummond-Moran, aged 28."

"Ugh, he looks a right typical leftie luvvie, doesn't he!" yelled Tidworth

"Just for the record, Sir, I am one of them," replied Ravi.

"Oh yes, well you are ok," said Tidworth in an insincerely apologetic voice.

"Anyway, what do we know about this Edmund Drummond-Moran person then?" asked Holloway.

"He was charged for damage to property in 2019. Drummond-Moran graffitied a Barclays Branch in Bristol with "murderers" during the 2019 Extinction Rebellion Protests. He was also involved in the 2020 Black Lives Matter protests and was arrested for breaching Public Health Regulations," remarked DC Jo Hardy.

"Oh, so he was one of those eco-loons. Firstly, I remember it was a scorcher of an Easter weekend then and I had to be on duty on London Bridge to try and keep those wacky-baccy people in order. Then, they ended up in my office. It was like a farmer dumped his dung heap in my office. I puked every time I went in there. Mind you, a dung heap would have more brains than them. And then those other protestors. They would smash up war memorials!"

"Mr Drummond-Moran didn't do that," replied Hardy.

"I saw one who did wreck a memorial and most of the police just stood there. I asked them why they let it happen. They said they didn't want to "hurt the protestors' feelings" and "put us at risk." Well, if they are smashing up memorials then I would happily do more to them than just "hurt their feelings." If they made me Chief Constable or Commissioner, which they won't because they know I can actually do my job properly, then I would purge ALL of those officers who said we should just stand back and let the violence happen. They say they don't want to handle risk. Oh bless! You don't join the force to act in *Heartbeat*! More idiots falling upwards and me climbing downwards."

"Anyway, how about Drummond-Moran's financial status?" enquired an increasingly exasperated Holloway.

"Well, he has been evicted before. His status appears to be improving after his shows with the Yasnaya Polyana theatre group, but I am not sure how he could buy a flat in Bloomsbury on that money." said DC Hardy, "It may be the case that there is money in his family. His father seems to own a lot of farms in Somerset and Dorset. Drummond-Moran went to Stowe then Cambridge where he read English but left after two years to concentrate on acting. He seemed to float around theatres in the South West. He lived in Totnes, Stroud and Bristol."

"Of course! Now it all becomes clear. Half those wacky baccy hippies were from Totnes. What is it about Totnes that attracts people who stink and dress like rotten veg?" sniped Tidworth.

"The Dartington College of Arts," interjected Holloway.

"So, it's a load of schoolkids?"

"No, it's an Arts college."

"Which means the people who go there are basically wasting their time?"

"Well, yes, but that's not what they think – my sister included."

Tidworth raised his eyebrows, curious at why the sister of a British Army officer was at this rather odd arts college, "oh so she is one of these radical hippy wacky baccies?"

"I wouldn't go that far, but we have, you know, debates. Can we talk about the suspects, not some random arts college," said Holloway, trying to stop Tidworth's tangents.

DS Chakravarty then put a picture of Drummond-Moran's partner, Elena Kuzmina, up on the whiteboard.

"Well, my god I bet she gets that thesp in order," commented Tidworth – nobody seemed to care at this point what his opinions were of the suspects.

"Kuzmina fled Russia in 2020 after she was arrested for participating in a demonstration against the prolongation of Vladimir Putin's presidency. She was an actress in a Moscow theatre for several years," said DC Hardy.

"Do you know anything else about her background?" asked Holloway.

"No, we don't. In fact, there is very little information about her except why she fled."

"Did she go to any colleges or universities?"

"She went to a theatre school in Moscow and graduated in 2010."

"Could you do some more background checking on her."

"Of course."

DS Chakravarty then started talking about Fred Mansfield, the theatre group's manager.

"He is an ex-actor but his record appears to be very bland. No financial problems. No connections to Russia. No criminal record."

Holloway and Tidworth went back to the DCI's office to have another private chat. They sat face to face and discussed the next course of action.

"It is not looking good for that Drummond-Moran bloke. We need to check him out," said Tidworth.

"He is perfect agent material. No money. Previous criminal record to be used as *kompromat*. There is one thing that puzzles me about his case. Drummond-Moran is starting to hit his prime and is getting success after some years. He spent all that time in obscurity, and he is getting roles on primetime TV now. I just went on my phone and saw he made a guest appearance in *Midsomer Murders*. Why throw it away now?"

"Perhaps he is trying to get over the shame of being on that dreadful show. That Barnaby bloke is so dopey if you know what I mean. He just trundles around in his Volvo, knocks on a cottage door, asks a couple of inane questions and cruises off in his Volvo."

Holloway rolled his eyes in response, "there is no need to be facetious! My point still stands. A few years ago, he was broke and jobbing around the West Country and now he is more stable and living in London, though I suppose it could be worth asking where he got his recent fame and fortune from."

DC Hardy came into the office to say that Edmund and Elena had booked to go to the Waddesdon Manor Autumn Fair that evening. Tidworth and Holloway decided to try and book themselves in too to find out about Edmund and Elena.

"Aha, only two spaces left sir," said Hardy.
"Well get a move on then," responded Tidworth with a bossy gesticulation.
Hardy was successful. Tidworth and Holloway were going to a funfair.

CHAPTER 2: THE MYSTERIOUS DISAPPEARING GYPSY

That afternoon Tidworth and Holloway set off for Waddesdon Manor in Buckinghamshire. Tidworth was going drive there in his white Jaguar coupe. Tidworth showed it off in the basement car park.

"There is one thing I go all mushy for and it is this baby!" remarked Tidworth with a wry smile, "I go all mushy for you don't I," whilst stroking the roof of his car like a dog.

"So this is what our taxes go on?" replied Holloway.

"Jeez, this is going to be a long journey," said Tidworth with a huff.

Whilst inevitably stuck in traffic somewhere on the M25 in pouring rain, Tidworth received a call from DC Hardy.

"I have been on the phone to the theatre school in Moscow, Elena Kuzmina was a student there when the database says she was. However, she died in 2011."

Holloway groaned, "oh no, it seems as if we might have two agents on our hands."

Tidworth was still rather flippant.

"What I am worried about is this traffic just won't move. Is everyone who owns a car in London a sloth?"

"I suspect most of them are wacky baccy hippies or hippy wacky baccies as you would say."

"Well, they are doing a good job of making me hate the M25. I miss the days of the Woodhead Pass. You could speed at 100 mph with beautiful scenery and now we are stuck near Heathrow Airport watching some planes!"

DS Chakravarty and DC Hardy went to the west London theatre where the Yasnaya Polyana theatre group were based for their latest show. They arrived in the Victorian reception of the theatre. There was a wrought iron canopy outside painted black and stained glass windows on the doors. The entrance hall on the other hand was rather dark and devoid of any colour. The carpet was a mottled dark red and the panelling in the room was dark oak. A rather unassuming, gaunt, balding man about six feet tall with a small goatee beard came to meet Chakravarty and Hardy in the entrance hall.

"So, Mr Mansfield. Where were you last night?" asked DS Chakravarty

"I was at home all the time. It was terrible what happened to Alexey and Yevgeniya," replied a clearly upset Mansfield

"Can anyone confirm your whereabouts?"

"My wife."

"I would like to ask you about Edmund Drummond-Moran and Elena Kuzmina," said DC Hardy, "what do you know about them?"

"Edmund is certainly an up-and-coming actor. He has been getting great reviews recently for several of his performances. We were really lucky to get him for our new play, premiering in a few days' time "The Cranes are Dying." Elena, I don't know much about her. She fled Russia a few years ago and has been trying to make her way in theatre world. She seems to be doing ok."

"Elena Kuzmina is not her real name though. She died in 2011."

Mansfield struggled to come up with answer at first and then said, "well, it is true that many dissidents change their names. She has probably done it for security reasons. As we have seen, London is a dangerous place for dissidents."

After sunset, Tidworth and Holloway arrived in the grounds of the Rothschild's imposing French Château, Waddesdon Manor, perched on a hill overlooking the Buckinghamshire country-side. They exited the car and entered the queue for temperature checks before going into the event. Tidworth received another phone call, this time from DS Chakravarty, about ballistics and his conversation with Mansfield.

"Sir, are you at the fair yet?"

"We eventually arrived. We have to have our temperature checked. The journey was horrible. I am sweating badly."

"Perhaps don't drive in your greatcoat," suggested Holloway.

"I didn't ask for your input Captain!"

Chakravarty told Tidworth about the details of the ballistics.

"Ok, so the calibre was 9mm."

Holloway asked about the length.

"It was 19mm," replied Chakravarty

"A Parabellum then. Could be from anywhere," said Holloway

"Ok on Fred Mansfield."

"Yes."

"He has an alibi for last night. His wife confirmed it. He seemed very normal and confirmed a lot of what we were saying earlier. Edmund is very much on the rise with his acting career after a lot of doldrums. Elena is still a mystery. His suggestion was that she uses a pseudonym for security reasons."

"Thanks for that, we shall find out more today."

Tidworth and Holloway arrived at the front of the fair queue. An attendant used a thermometer gun on them. Tidworth, for once, looked terrified with his mouth constantly open. Both of them passed although Tidworth's was rather high according to the attendant.

"Damn," Tidworth cursed, "I should have taken some paraceta-mol. Keeps the temperature down."

"DCI Tidworth bending the rules. Colour me shocked."

"There but for the grace of God goes God!"

"I wouldn't expect you to be so erudite."

"Winston Churchill apparently said it. His book of insults is a lifesaver when dealing with people like you."

Tidworth and Holloway walked up the torchlit one-way path towards the fair. The fires gave the setting the feel of being on a medieval camp. The fires were the only thing that kept the two of them warm in the crisp Autumn evening air. Entering the funfair itself was like going back in time too. The sound of organ pipes playing waltzes, the white carnival lights, the smell of cinnamon spice and hot chocolate in the air and 19th century font throughout the fair gave it a nostalgic and romantic feel. Many events over the last few years had adapted to this new outdoor lifestyle and Waddesdon Manor was no exception. Everyone seemed to be laughing and enjoying themselves. Tidworth and Holloway had been transported to a different world. Waddesdon was a far cry from the threatening yet mundane existence of London.

Holloway spotted their targets – Edmund Drummond-Moran and Elena Kuzmina – having some hot chocolate at a food stall. They both fitted in well with the retro settings. Edmund was wearing a vintage great coat with a scarf. His short black hairstyle also made him look like a character from another time too. Elena was wearing a long fur coat and a large round hat with fair hair in a bob. They seemed yet another example that the fair was a dreamworld. Two people who did not seem like they existed in the real world.

Holloway said that he had been looking up Drummond-Moran's acting career on his phone. His plan was to fanboy Drummond-Moran and to try and get into a conversation about his acting career. Tidworth had another idea. Next to the food stall was an air rifle shooting game. He saw that as a good aptitude test for who might be an agent. Tidworth and Holloway were highly suspicious of both of them. Edmund the actor who needs some money and Elena who doesn't exist.

Holloway minced up to Edmund and Elena with an embarrassed

smirk on his face.

"Aha, so you are Edmund Drummond-Moran. I remember I saw you in a play in Exeter a few years ago. You played Meursault in a stage adaptation of *L'Étranger*. You were so convincing. I remember, you did it because of the sun. Can I have your signature please?"

"Of course, you have good cultural tastes mon ami. Meursault was my big break it has been onwards and upwards from then on. I even made a guest appearance on *Midsomer Murders* last year!" in a campish public schoolboy accent.

Edmund got his pen out to sign Holloway's note pad.

"Who should I address this to?" asked Edmund.

"Call me Tim."

"*Namaste* Tim," said Edmund with his hands together and a bow. "Best wishes for Tim from Edmund Drummond-Moran. All done."

"By the way, what happened when you appeared in *Midsomer Murders*?"

"Basically, I died in the first 10 minutes."

"How?"

"I drowned in a yoghurt vat."

"Do you think the writers are starting to run out of ideas in how to murder people?"

"Probably, but it was absolutely such fun to be swimming around in a massive container of yoghurt."

Holloway wanted to find out more about the Yasnaya Polyana theatre group. Meanwhile, Tidworth was in the background trying to get a go on the air rifle shooting range.

"So, what are you doing at the minute?" asked Holloway

"Basically, I am part of this theatre group that is made up of people who have fled Putin's Russia like my friend Elena here. It is called the Yasnaya Polyana Theatre Group – named after Tolstoy's house. She is an actress and she will be performing in our new play with me "The Cranes are Dying." I, naturally, am the lead," Edmund replied

"Wonderful, are you friends?"

"Oh yes, very much," Edmund said with emphasis and an impish smile before having a quick hug with Elena.

"He is very nice to me. Frankly speaking, I was lost when I escaped from Russia three years ago, but thanks to him, I am fulfilling my dream of, as you English say, 'treading the boards,'" said Elena.

"What is this new play about?"

"It is based on a film from the 1950s called "The Cranes are Flying,"" remarked Edmund.

"Aha, I see what you did there!" joked Holloway in an attempt to get the pun. He had heard of the film when learning Russian, but he had never watched it.

"Basically, it is the tragic story of two lovers, Boris and Veronika, during World War One in Russia. It is an examination of the dangers of jingoistic nationalism which I believe we are seeing a dangerous resurgence of in this country and in the west in general. I am playing Boris. Pun kind of intended," explained Edmund with his inane sense of humour.

"And I am playing Veronika," said Elena with an excited screech. Holloway had the look of someone who had eaten a raw lemon after what he perceived to be Edmund's left-wing internationalist proselytizing.

Tidworth came along into the conversation with two air rifles. He threw one of them at Edmund who dropped it.

"What's all this about? Who are you?" said Edmund looking totally shocked with his jaw dropping.

"I am Len, err, um, err, um Tim's boss. We are going to play a little game. We are going to shoot at these targets. Whoever gets the most points wins a teddy bear. Me versus you thesp. Err, um, err, um Tim versus the Russian bird. Let's go for it!" exclaimed Tidworth who could hardly contain his excitement for getting his hands on a gun.

The first round was Tidworth vs Edmund. At the brightly lit

yellow and red stall, Tidworth almost hit the middle of the target. Edmund, firing with a front-on posture, hit one of the teddy bears after the rifle butt kicked back into his shoulder.

"Ahhh! I think I will need to see my osteopath tomorrow!" shrieked Edmund whilst clutching his shoulder.

"No, what you need my friend is to get a professional on the job. Me! I will show you what I used to do to my recruits in the military," before grabbing Edmund's shoulder, yanking it and popping it like a Chiropractor. Edmund's face was even more startled than before.

Next was Elena versus Holloway. Holloway scored 7 out of 10. Elena's shooting posture seemed very professional. It showed, she hit the middle of the target – closer than Tidworth.

"Well, that was a fix wasn't it? Mind you, the Russians always cheat. You are probably taking an inhaler or something like that," huffed Tidworth.

"No, the English Army is not what it used to be," said Elena in a smarmy voice full of schadenfreude.

The couples parted on acrimonious terms with Elena taking the teddy bear. The Tidworth and Holloway couple were spitting blood at each other.

"You are brilliant at HUMINT aren't you DCI Tidworth. You even used your own name and said you were in the Army. She saw right through you," exclaimed Holloway.

"HUMINT? I'm starting to lose the acronyms, know what I mean."

"Going undercover."

"Well, I never needed to go undercover because I am skilled enough to manage without it."

"Wow! That is what you call complacency."

"And all you do is sit behind a desk looking at screens whilst I have actually had to face people like the IRA," responded an even more irritated Tidworth, pointing his finger at his junior colleague.

Tailing Edmund and Elena was very difficult. Tidworth and Holloway had to hide behind some stalls if they came close. At one point, the couple were on a galloper carousel and the two investigators cowered behind a candy floss stall to stop being spotted. Then, Elena and Edmund entered the gypsy soothsayer tent of 'Mr Stokowski.' The tent was like a mini circus big top with yellow and red stripes down the side of it. Holloway and Tidworth observed from the coconut shy stall.

Inside the tent, Edmund and Elena sat down and met 'Mr Stokowski.' The 'gypsy' had a scar down the left-hand side of his face and a bushy black moustache and was dressed in a white flannel shirt with a cravat. He smelt as if he had just consumed several raw garlic cloves – Edmund grimaced disapprovingly at the scents. The room was dark except for a little oil lamp at Stokowski's little wooden table on top of a large Persian rug. There was an electric heater in the tent to try and keep it warm. Nonetheless, the tent was still cold enough for condensation to steam up the room whenever someone spoke. 'Mr Stokowski' read Edmund's palm after putting some hand sanitiser on.
"You are going to have a big show in a week's time, and it will be very successful," Stokowski said in a very thick, if hammy, Eastern European accented English.
He had a conversation with Elena in Russian – a language that Edmund did not understand - though he did recognise a word that sounded something like "premiere." He looked startled at the conversation. He was suspicious as to why Elena and this gypsy were talking for so long but did not ask any questions.

After Elena and Edmund left the tent, Tidworth and Holloway entered. They saw and heard nothing except for a few strangled groans. A short, thin man wearing clothes that looked like they were brought from a vintage clothing store was curled up like a baby and gagged in a corner so dark it would have been impossible to notice him in the first place. Holloway ripped a sack off his head to reveal a black-haired man in his 50s who had a bushy

16

black moustache. This little man also, just smelt of garlic. He described what happened to Holloway and Tidworth.

"My word, if Count Dracula entered this tent, he would be dead in seconds!" exclaimed Tidworth with his hand over his nose.

"My name is Mr Stokowski and some time ago, I was hit over the head by a man who entered from behind. I have only just woken up. There were some people here a short time ago. I heard voices. What is the time? Oh, it is half past seven. I have missed several clients," he said in a croaky and groggy voice whilst staggering up.

"So presumably you can't describe who hit you over the head?" asked Holloway.

"Unfortunately, I can't."

"What about the voices. What did they sound like?"

Mr Stokowski, now seated at his table, was struggling to marshal his memory.

"There were two men, one was definitely English and the other I believe was speaking Russian to a Russian-speaking woman I believe."

"Did you understand what they were saying."

"In reality, I am Romanian. My name is not Stokowski, it is Andrei Petrescu and I am pretending to be a gypsy. I did learn some Russian when I was a child, but I have forgotten it. I can only recognise it."

"Thank you, that has been very helpful."

In the meantime, Tidworth had gone out to get an icepack for Mr Stokowski's head. When he came back in through the curtain door. Mr Stokowski exclaimed.

"Thank you very much sir. Now would you like me to read *your* hand?"

"Not over my dead body. Get that ice pack on your head now. Come on, we're going Holloway."

Tidworth left in a huff with Holloway. They made their way out of the fair along the torchlit path.

"What did you think of that, Len?"

"I am not getting into any of that snake oily stuff. No, no, no! Someone in my family used to be obsessed with Ouija Boards and all that type of rubbish and it was just rubbish. Absolute rubbish. Doesn't mean anything. Stokowski or whatever he is called is only doing it cause otherwise he would be scrounging off benefits. Mind you, he probably is anyway."

"He was quite helpful to us though."

"Yeah, I suppose."

"The gypsy who hit him over the head wanted to talk to Edmund and Elena for a reason. They were at the fair for a reason. We need to find out why. We need to bring one of them in and play them off against each. That 'gypsy' was probably their handler."

Tidworth and Holloway got into their car at the car park at the bottom of the hill. Tidworth revved up the engine to about 3000 to 4000 RPM and they shot off back to London.

CHAPTER 3: ENSNAREMENT

12th October 2023

Edmund Drummond-Moran woke up in the flat he shared with Elena Kuzmina in Bloomsbury. It was in a Georgian terrace over-looking a square lined with lime trees. The square had a green in the middle where a small coffee kiosk was always parked. That morning, at about 8am, he left his flat to get a coffee, with almond milk, a pastry and a newspaper, always *The Guardian*, across the square at the kiosk.

Wearing the same great coat that he wore at Waddesdon and a tartan scarf, he strode up to the kiosk to get his "usual." The Indian kiosk server, Ramesh, chatted away to him about the latest local news from the rustic caravan kiosk.

"Keir Starmer came here yesterday," Ramesh said in a smug voice.

"Oh did he! I do see him around sometimes."

"He asked for an Americano and wondered why there was no milk in it. Not so forensic."

"Well, he is surely more forensic than who-must-not-be-named slash the terrible Winston Churchill impersonator. Remember, I always have almond milk."

"Of course, mate."

Edmund got his coffee, a cinnamon swirl, a newspaper and sat on a nearby bench. He perched right on the edge of the bench with his usual very straight posture, always rolling his shoul-ders. He was so far forward on the bench that he almost slipped off the front of it. All seemed very peaceful and content as he read what their columnists thought about the world. Edmund was content whilst reading an investigation into Boris Johnson's meetings with an unknown Russian oligarch whilst on holiday in Italy.

Behind him, a man and a woman both in Balaclavas with knives came up to him and threatened him.
"Come with us or we shall slit your throat," they said whilst one held their knife to his neck and the other grabbed him.
In shock, Edmund dropped his coffee and spilt it on his coat.
"I got that coat when I went to Bicester Village. It is very special to me. Let me go!"

His appeals to fashion were to no avail. The man put a hood over him and the woman bound his hands before being taken to a black Mercedes people carrier with tinted windows. They snatched his phone and wallet. Whilst writhing, he was thrown on the back seat of the van and it sped off with its wheels screeching.

In a basement car park somewhere in East London, Edmund was transferred to a saloon car which drove him to a hangar at an abandoned airfield in the south of the city. It was a dark and dank aircraft junkyard full of old airliners from the decimated airline industry. International air travel was still in the process of a struggling rehabilitation from a tremendous battering. Big, empty shells stood as an eerie testament to a lost time.

The two kidnappers took Edmund into the hangar. In the middle was a small table with two chairs at one side and one on the other. The only lighting was a white 1980s-style desk lamp on the table.

The kidnappers ripped off the blindfold and cut the bonding to reveal DCI Tidworth in his suit and greatcoat and Captain Holloway in camouflage with a cypress green beret sitting on the other side of the table. Since it was October, Holloway was wearing long rather than short sleeves. It was just one of those unquestioning idiosyncratic conventions the Army had. As Tennyson would have said, their's not to make reply, their's not to reason why, their's but to do and die (of heat exhaustion or a chill). The cold morning made the long sleeves bearable though.

"I have seen you two before," said a startled Edmund after about a ten second pause.
"You have Edmund. I am Captain Daniel Holloway of the Army Intelligence Corps and this is my colleague from the Metropolitan Police Counter Terrorism Division DCI Len Tidworth. I have made you a coffee with almond milk. Plus, here is a pastry and today's Guardian," explained Holloway whilst handing Edmund his usual start to the day. Tidworth seemed a bit insulted to be referred to merely as a "colleague."

Holloway explained that since the day after the funfair, he and Tidworth had put Edmund under surveillance. 'Ramesh' was DS Chakravarty undercover wearing a beard. DC Hardy was one of the kidnappers and a detective from a different division was the other. The plan was to do a fake kidnap and mugging of Edmund rather than simply bringing him in for questioning. If he was taken to Tidworth's office for questioning, the spy ring's suspicions would be raised greatly. At least this fake abduction and mugging would be look less conspicuous. DC Hardy took his wallet and phone in the van.

Holloway began interrogating Edmund about his girlfriend. Chucking a picture of Elena onto the table, Holloway asked, "who is this?"
With a 'well, duh' type of expression, Edmund replied, "it is my girlfriend, Elena Kuzmina."
"Tell us what you know about her."
"She fled Russia in 2020 when protesting against Putin's attempt to become President for life. She told me how she escaped on the back of a truck headed for Finland and how she was nearly captured."

"So, what do you know about her life and education?"

"She went to a prestigious Moscow theatre school and was in many productions at theatres throughout Russia."

"Elena Kuzmina did go to that theatre school and graduated in 2010."

"Yes, she did. That's what she said," replied Edmund in yet another 'well duh' style.

"*That* Elena Kuzmina died in 2011," said Holloway gravely, as if he was delivered news of a bereavement to Edmund.

"What!" shrieked Edmund with his hands over his gaping mouth before going for a stroll around to try and understand the situation. "What does this mean? Why are you interested in this?"

DCI Tidworth then took over the questioning.

"Alexey Ostrovsky and Yevgeniya Tikhonova – did I say that right Captain?" he said gesticulating towards Holloway

"Yes, you did," replied Holloway with a nod.

"They were found dead in an industrial estate in East London a few nights ago. Each with a bullet in the back of their heads. It looked like an organised killing. As they were prominent dissidents and vocal critics of the Putin regime, it would not surprise me if the order to kill them came from Moscow. There has been a trend in the last few years, from Skripal to Navalny, of the Russian secret service bumping off people it doesn't like abroad. We think that this is not over yet. You live with somebody who is not who she says she is. We need hard evidence that she is connected to these murders somehow."

Edmund, still startled and dawdling about the hangar, was, uncharacteristically lost for words.

"On the night of the 7 and 8th October, where was Elena?"

"In bed."

"For the whole time?"

"For the time that I was awake, yes."

"But she could have left whilst you were asleep."

"I would have probably woken up if she did."

"The time of death we think was somewhere between 1 am and 2 am on the 8th. Can you confirm that Elena Kuzmina or whoever she is was in your flat?"

"No, I was definitely asleep at midnight."

"That means she has no alibi for that night."

Holloway took over the interrogation again and moved onto the gypsy tent at the funfair.

"We saw you and Elena go into the gypsy tent of Mr Stokowski. What happened when you were in there?"

Edmund sat down again before starting his answers.

"Basically, the gypsy read my hand and said my upcoming show, which I have to rehearse for soon by the way, would be a success. Then he and Elena started talking Russian. I don't understand the language, but I heard the word "premiere" referring to our play "The Cranes are Dying""

"Could you describe what he looked like."

"Big black bushy moustache. Wore old and flamboyant clothes. Yes, yes, yes, why am I so stupid," he exclaimed whilst banging the table.

"What have you realised?"

"He had a scar down the left-hand side of his face. Last night, myself and Elena went to a nearby park where she met an exiled homeless painter called 'Mikhail' and he too had the same scar. Elena and he were talking Russian."

"The same scar?"

"Yes."

"The exact same one?"

"Yes."

"Because we found the real 'Mr Stokowski' and he did not have a scar. He had been incapacitated by an unknown assailant. It seems as if this gypsy and the homeless painter wanted to talk to Elena and not you. This suggests that she has some sort of role in the killings. We need to find more evidence. We have jigsaw pieces but not a picture."

"What do you propose?"

Tidworth then spoke about his plan.

"The plan is to look at your bins."

"You seriously don't think *I* would rummage around in my own bins."

"I don't expect people like you would ever dream of doing it."

"Well, no, because I have hygiene standards," replied Edmund with the grimace of someone who has just picked up a rotten banana.

"Told you he was a lightweight!" said Tidworth with a wicked grin towards Holloway.

"Do not call me a lightweight," moaned Edmund like a teenager

"Well, *you* can get your hands dirty in your bins, not me."

"Ok, deal done, you can look through my bins," said Edmund in a defensive fashion

"When is she out?"

"Tomorrow night between 5 and 7pm she has a Krav Maga class."

"What's Krav Maga?" quizzed Tidworth with a befuddled squint.

"An Israeli martial art."

"I bet she wouldn't last a minute against me in a bust-up. So, between 5 and 7, we will have a look through your bins."

"You said that about the shooting a few nights ago. By the way, the park where I met the painter is called Chamberlain Park."

"We shall check out the CCTV for the park. Remember, arrive back at your house with a limp. You want to look like you have *actually* been mugged," explained Holloway

"I have been murdered in *Midsomer Murders,* so I know how to look injured."

"Nah! They're not *proper* murders," cackled Tidworth.

"I drowned in a vat of yoghurt."

"See, I told you. I have been doing this job for 15-20 years and I have *never* seen anyone drown in a vat of yoghurt or get knocked over the head with some cheese."

"What about my phone and wallet?"

"You will get them back tomorrow," said Holloway

"Just as nice as when I got arrested in Bristol in 2019. You are so generous."

"By the way, you smell nice for one of those wacky baccy hippies!" shouted Tidworth

"I left them a few year ago and I wear Eau de Cologne every day."

"Get him in the car!" exclaimed Tidworth just as Edmund was bundled back into the boot of the saloon which drove out of the hangar so fast it almost crashed. Edmund arrived back at his flat in Bloomsbury with a limp and missing his phone and wallet. He told Elena about how he had been mugged. Now, it was his turn for revenge. She had been lying to him for three years, so this deception seemed like poetic justice.

CHAPTER 4: THE INQUISITIVE BINMEN

13th October 2023

Holloway and Tidworth, dressed in white overalls with N95 masks and surgical gloves, turned up at Edmund's flat to rummage through the bins at 5pm prompt.

"You look like somebody out of Ghostbusters," said Edmund who answered the door with a colourful blue shirt and tight chinos.

"And you look like somebody from Brighton!" grunted Tidworth.

"Ok, Edmund, show us where the bins are. Here is your wallet and phone," said Holloway.

Edmund put his greatcoat on after putting his belongings back in his pocket and took the two white suited men round the back of the terrace.

"Do you want anything to drink?"

"I know I am from t'other side of Pennines, but I only drink Yorkshire tea. Only Yorkshire tea at the minute. No coffee any time after lunch," said Tidworth.

"Urgh, that's cheap stuff. I always have loose leaf green tea in the evenings," replied Edmund with disgust.

"I will take Green Tea if it is on offer Edmund, but nothing too fancy please," said Holloway.

"Of course, and you, my friend, will take an odyssey with tea. Maybe a jasmine blend?"

"I have never been so terrified of anything but a terrible cup of tea," said a visibly nervous Tidworth.

Tidworth and Holloway started their search after they got their

teas – which Tidworth spat out immediately in the direction of his colleague. Holloway pulled a face as if he had drunk petrol.
"I can't drink this. It tastes like my wife's perfume!" the policeman moaned whilst shaking his head in utter disgust.

They were looking for shreddings, photos or anything else that may provide information about Kuzmina. Holloway struck gold with something quite early on. The masks were a good idea. The bins were full of very fancy food that was going off.
"This is a ripped-up photograph of some soldiers. Jesus Christ! Look at this Len. You see that woman in combat gear on the far right of the photo. That is her. Can you just about make out the logo?"
"Yeah, it is a bat on her arm."
"GRU Spetsnatz."
"Jeez."
"You see the flag? It is the Donetsk People's Republic. There is snow on the ground. This must be the winter of 2014/5. I spent my gap year volunteering in eastern Ukraine, Donetsk Oblast. That winter was very cold."
"This is like Skripal all over again. If you put a bit of backbone and trawl through some stuff, you can find them out. It amazes me how sloppy these people are."

The rummage continued. This time, Tidworth found what looked like cut-up official diplomatic documents.
"Obviously you will be needed to translate these. I can't read them."
"Ok, it is addressed to Major Yekaterina Sokolova. It wishes her good luck in London. It talks about an operation called 'Cherry Orchard.' These documents and photos have all been shredded recently since they are in the bin at the minute."
"It seems very sloppy to be carrying around paper documents. Why not use WhatsApp, it's pretty secure people tell me."
"Paper is even safer, as long as you know how to dispose of it."
"So what does this mean? Are we meant to see this?

"Good question. But say it is genuine, these documents suggest she may be a) worried her cover might be blown, b) there is a big risky operation coming up or c) she might be coming to the end of an assignment and is destroying anything to do with it. Now Edmund mentioned that she said something about a premiere of the play he is acting in tomorrow. We have to inform him. If she is coming to the end of her assignment, she may want to destroy anything that is a record of what she did. That means Edmund could be in danger."

"The bigger question is: will the powers that be let us do something about this?"

Edmund came out soon after to collect the dirty cups.

"How did you find it?"

"Rubbish," replied Tidworth.

"We do have some very bad news," said Holloway in a subdued voice.

"Don't worry, not everybody likes green tea," replied Edmund who seemed totally oblivious to the situation.

"You know how we said that your girlfriend was not really Elena Kuzmina."

"Mmhmm."

"We have found out who she really is..."

"And."

"Her name is Major Yekaterina Sokolova. She has been a member of an elite GRU Spetsnaz unit and is currently a spy for the Russian government. To be exact, the GRU is an intel agency attached to the Russian military and it has been involved in election interference in the USA and the Skripal poisoning in Salisbury a few years ago." Edmund was looking totally deflated at the minute knowing he had been duped for the last three years. "There is a picture here showing her in Eastern Ukraine in 2014/5. Sokolova it seems was tasked with infiltrating the Yasnaya Polyana Theatre Group to find and kill Russian dissident exiles here in London. It seems as if the deaths of Ostrovsky and Tikhonova were part of the plan. They trusted her and then she killed them."

"What does this mean for me?"

"She is going to want to erase everything of her assignment here. The greatest weapon any intel agency could have to find her out in the future is you. You, Edmund, know her better than anyone who we know exists on this planet. You know her personality, her fads, her looks, her hobbies, her routine. Even though you didn't know who she *really* was, you still know more than any of us in intel and security. I think that she is going to be finishing her assignment soon, probably at the premiere of your play, and the way to tip it off is to get rid of you. That way, nobody in the future can really know who Yekaterina Sokolova was."

Edmund was visibly shaken by the announcement and almost dropped the cups.

"So, you are saying that I could be dead in about 24 hours. I did a dress rehearsal today and it all seemed so normal. My world has been turned upside down, but I am thankful that I know who she really is," said Edmund who by this point was visibly welling up.

"Do not do anything rash in the next 24 hours. There are probably others out there. We shall be parked very near your house. Our officers, including myself, will be keeping close surveillance of your house. We shall give you a burner phone. Also, I think it would be a good idea if I was an extra in your play."

"Yes, that sounds a wonderful idea. Thank you so much. You can be a Russian peasant."

"Wonderful. So, for the next 24 hours, try to stay as close to 'normal' as you can. As an actor, you are probably the best person to do this. Could I have some hand gel please."

"Of course."

Holloway rubbed some hand gel on and did a fist bump with Edmund before going. Tidworth reminded him that next time, he needed to have some Yorkshire tea.

Edmund knew that Tidworth and Holloway would be encamped in their car close by and that 'Ramesh' (DS Chakravarty really) would be in the kiosk. Nonetheless, he couldn't stop tapping his feet on the floor, biting his nails and twiddling his fingers. When 'Elena' came back from her class, she found him at his desk going through his lines.

"How did the Krav Maga go?"

"Very good thank you. You should try it some time with me. Might be good for your stage combat."

"Haha, no thank you," he replied in a subdued fashion.

When she went to bed, she tried to call him up.

"Are you coming up Edmund?"

"Erm, no, I am a little bit too nervous to sleep. I will stay down here. It is my big day tomorrow."

He carried on reading his lines knowing he may never get to use them.

CHAPTER 5: THE CRANES ARE DYING

At seven in the morning on the next day, Holloway was walking along the path with two coffees and two takeaway cooked breakfasts in biodegradable plastic containers. He and Tidworth had been staking out Edmund's house for a few hours and came to get refreshments. Tidworth had hired a black BMW so as to have a less conspicuous stake out car. Since it was still not light yet in London, Holloway had some difficulty finding the car in the dank and misty square. After about five minutes of flailing around the square and the park Holloway opened to door to give Tidworth his breakfast. As Holloway sat in the car and passed the DCI his food, Tidworth remarked with a concerned expression,

"I hope that hasn't gone cold," remarked a perturbed Tidworth

"It's in a packet," Holloway replied

"Yeah, that's the problem. It's that eco-guff," the DCI said with disgust. Tidworth opened the box sheepishly and grimaced at the contents before pushing them around with his cardboard cutlery.

"What?" said Holloway with a smattering of dread whilst turning to Tidworth.

"I told you I wanted the full works. So, what do I have? Poached egg, mushrooms, spinach, tomato, some Swiss potato thing all covered in some green sludge, which I think, and hope, is avocado, and," whilst pointing his finger at the breakfast as if he was arguing with it, "it is topped with chilli seeds. This is the kind of muck that Edward would cook up, if he could even cook,"

"You mean Edmund."

"Huh."

"Anyway, it's better than the stuff I get given, and you used to get, in the Army."

"No, it's worse."

"Really? The rations always look like they have just been puked up."

"Yeah, and this is even worse than the stuff we'd get in Sarajevo. It's going in the bin! I suppose it won't suffocate any turtles with this 'eco' material."

Tidworth got out of the car and slammed the door closed whilst huffing. He walked right up to the closest bin and threw the breakfast package at it with such force and contempt that he missed.

He stomped back to the car in a huff and slammed the door shut when he sat back down.

"It's not your fault, it's the city's. It's almost like it doesn't belong in this country, know what I mean. We should drive somewhere that actually does a fry up. You shouldn't have bothered with this area."

Holloway saw Edmund leaving his house for breakfast and nudged the policeman to alert him. They got out of the car and tailed him as he walked to the kiosk. Edmund seemed to be walking with urgency and looking behind him all the time. His pace and gait was that of a quick march. Despite trying to keep their distance from him, Holloway and Tidworth realised that Edmund probably knew he was being followed by them. They sheepishly stopped behind a tree as the actor brought his breakfast, intermittently taking glances at Edmund. However, a female eastern European voice coming from behind them made Holloway and Tidworth jump.

"I know you said you were big fans but isn't this called stalking over here?" said an inquisitive Yekaterina.

Tidworth looked ready to say something to the Russian agent. Holloway, dreading that this rash move would lead to disaster quickly butted in with an explanation.

32

"We are showbiz journalists for *Lorraine*, so it is kind of our job to stalk celebrities."

"Journalists!" replied Yekaterina with an eye roll and tut, "They are terrible. The showbiz ones are the worst. The political ones would at least do a daring investigation into police incompetence, you just want to find out my breast size. Happy hunting!"

She walked back to her home with a smirk and a nod at Tidworth and Holloway.

Holloway and Tidworth had made a flustered retreat back to the car.

"She knows doesn't she," said Holloway with an anxious tone to his voice.

"Yeah," replied an equally agitated Tidworth.

"How did she know?"

"Hopefully intuition. You aren't from the police - she at least got that wrong."

"You don't think he told her?"

"If he did that, he's even more stupid than we think."

"Surely she would have killed him for that…unless the 'Edmund' we saw was a body double."

Tidworth sat back in his chair, looked up to the ceiling and ruminated for a couple of seconds.

"Nah, she would've bumped him off for grassing. I think you're overthinking it," Tidworth replied dismissively.

"What do you think we should do next?"

Tidworth let out a heavy exhalation before answering.

"I think we have to have a crisis meeting. By the way, did you gain approval to go undercover at the theatre?"

"No," replied Holloway with a shrug of his shoulders, "should I?"

"It's the way things are unfortunately. I wouldn't be surprised if paperwork and bureaucracy has cost more lives in this city than knives and guns."

An emergency meeting took place back at Tidworth's office. In the room along with the DCI was Holloway, DS Chakravarty and

DC Hardy. Tidworth's superior, Superintendent Julia Watkins, joined the meeting via Microsoft Teams. Tidworth sat at the end of the table in the prosaic office, Holloway on Tidworth's right and Chakravarty and Hardy on his left. Watkins was on a monitor facing Tidworth at the end of an empty mahogany table, dressed in a black and white uniform with a union flag behind her left shoulder. She had very short cropped grey hair, wore black spectacles on her nose and glared at the camera. Her expression looked as if she disapproved of Tidworth's plans before he even opened his mouth. There were no pleasantries when the conversation started.

Tidworth began the conversation by outlining his plan to protect Edmund from Yekaterina Sokolova.

"We have reason to believe that Edmund-Drummond Moran will be killed by his girlfriend slash GRU agent by the end of the day," said Tidworth in an uncharacteristically timid and deferential voice. Superintendent Watkins furiously scribbled in her notepad, looking up at the DCI with a scowl intermittently.

Tidworth continued, "I propose we send Captain Daniel Holloway, sitting here to my right, undercover as an extra at the premiere of Mr Drummond-Moran's play tonight."

"Yes, I saw that you found her identity," replied the Superintendent curtly.

"She is also guilty of the murders of the Russian dissidents a few days ago."

"I think that is for the CPS to decide," said Watkins dismissively.

"We need to snatch her before she runs away, which I think will be imminent. Her mission is over."

Watkins noted Tidworth's comments down in her notebook. She made a furious scribble before making her reply.

"If her mission is over, why will she kill Mr Drummond-Moran?" the superintendent probed.

Tidworth looked glum as he prepared to answer Watkins's question.

"So, err, well, the, err, there was a err letter," Tidworth stuttered whilst Watkins shook her head in disbelief.

Watkins interrupted, "I know what this is about. You don't need to waffle. You have ruffled their feathers and they are going to strike back."

"You haven't even heard what my plan is yet!" a clearly irritated Tidworth hit back.

"I don't need to. Because it will be too dangerous whatever it is!" replied Watkins, shouting like an angry primary school teacher telling off her delinquent pupils.

The mood in Tidworth's meeting room was a mixture of frustration, resignation and dread. Frustration because Holloway, Tidworth, Chakravarty and Hardy felt they were being let down by their superiors who had little skin in the game. Resignation because they knew there was little to be gained from disobeying their superiors. Dread because they knew that following orders would lead to Edmund's death.

Tidworth tried one last heave against Superintendent Watkins's obstinacy.

"I am unhappy because you are doing all you can to sabotage my plans. I am angry because you don't even have the nerve to tell me I am wrong to my face. You just whinge and whine like a spoilt and bitter teenager behind your computer screen."

Watkins scowled in response and said very glumly, "you know the consequences of speaking to people like that."

"I don't bloody care! You don't deserve my respect! It is people like you who tell us to bang up those who want us to do our job and tell us to kneel to those who want us not to have a job. People like you will run us into the ground. I bet you want us to be so incompetent that everyone actually wants the police to get defunded!"

Tidworth hit the red button on Microsoft Teams to end the conversation. Everyone else stared at Tidworth as if nuclear war had just broken out. In response, the DCI nonchalantly shrugged his shoulders to suggest 'what else could I have done?'

After the explosive video conference with Superintendent Watkins, Holloway sought out Tidworth in his office. The DCI was sitting at his desk chomping Walkers cheese and onion crisps with his mouth open so you could the white pulpish remains of the potatoes. Holloway grimaced and gagged as he walked into the poorly ventilated small office.

A peeved off Tidworth said "what? What is it? Is it about what I said? That's hardly the worst thing I have said to anyone."

"No," replied Holloway who almost looked like he was having an anaphylactic shock, coughing uncontrollably into his elbow

"I have a bag of peanuts in here. The army obviously missed something when they let you in."

Holloway shook his head whilst coughing his guts out.

Tidworth started to look crestfallen. "Oh no," he said with a sense of paranoid foreboding, "no-one's poisoned you have they?"

"No," said Holloway who was breathing heavily and getting his voice back after his coughing fit, "could you please open the windows. Those crisps smell ghastly!"

Holloway finally sat down opposite Tidworth and they began to discuss a course of action.

"So it's off then?" remarked a disappointed Holloway, leaning forwards with hunched shoulders.

"Yes and no," replied Tidworth.

Holloway leant back in his chair and his posture became much more erect as if the tone of the conversation had become more positive.

"What do you suggest then? I am happy to go into the theatre this afternoon but are your superiors?" asked the British Army Captain.

"Sod them. You just do your own thing. I will make sure you will have support. It won't be ideal I will make sure it's there if you need it."

"Thanks, this opportunity is the only one we've got to beat Sokolova before she leaves. Whatever the cost, we have got to get in that theatre tonight."

Holloway knew that he was going on a dangerous mission. Physically dangerous because he would be on his own most of the time against Sokolova. Professionally dangerous too because he and Tidworth were going rogue. Nonetheless, he knew that a good officer should be prepared to make sacrifices and to challenge sub-optimal authority. Captain Holloway rushed out of the office to the theatre to check if Edmund Drummond-Moran was still alive.

At about 14:00, five and a half hours before the start, Holloway arrived at the theatre to dress up as an extra. In the red curtained dressing room, Edmund showed Holloway the brown rags, flat cap and the beard he would be wearing for the play. Holloway would also be wearing a mouthguard to make his character seem toothless. The flaw with this mouthguard was that it would hamper his speech. However, Sokolova would hopefully not recognise him. After Holloway travelled back in time to Imperial Russia in 1914, Edmund came back to see how he was doing. He pranced into the dressing room wearing black trousers, an almost dandy-like shirt, a waistcoat and a black Victorian-esque tie.
"Oh, you are looking rather gorgeous in that costume," remarked Edmund with a smirk.
"I may be toothless, but I am armed with a pitchfork," Holloway grunted whilst pretending to threaten Edmund with the pitchfork.
"Very good, perhaps you should do some more shows with us."
"Good thing is you seem remarkably sprightly for someone in your situation."
"I just have to concentrate on the show and hopefully everything will be fine," replied Edmund, grimacing to put a brave face on his predicament.
The two went on stage for the final dress rehearsal. Holloway watched the first scene from a side entrance to the stage as Edmund and Sokolova's characters talked to each other in a sitting room. His heartbeat shot up when Sokolova picked up a small and sharp ice hammer to make some drinks. She briefly brandished this would-be weapon around, as if she was preparing to

throw it. Holloway's breathing got even quicker. He grabbed a copy of the script to see if the ice pick was part of the performance. Scrambling through the pages, he went too far into the script at first before flicking back so violently that Edmund and Sokolova may have heard his flailing. Holloway knew that if he was acting suspiciously and Sokolova heard him, there could be two victims of the ice pick that afternoon. Finally, he found the right page and, to his relief, Sokolova was supposed to pick up an ice hammer.

Thankfully, no-one was killed in the dress rehearsal. Holloway was more concerned that he had no idea what exactly was going on in the play. Firstly, the storyline was non-linear. The first act was set in the summer of 1914, the second in December 1916, the Third in the 1760s, the fourth in 1573 and the fifth in 2199 which, in the same act, flashed back to December 1916 then forwards again to 2199. The choice of dates, except those set in World War One, all seemed rather random. The story had no flow whatsoever, instead it was a clump of vignettes which created an over-arching intellectual narrative. The final scene of the play saw about 30 naked extras walking onto the stage where red paint was poured over all of them and they fell on the floor screaming in blood-curdling agony. The plain white walls of the set and the whole stage floor was splattered with red paint. Holloway and Edmund were observing this absurd and satanic scene from the side entrance. Edmund was dressed in World War One Russian uniform with a tin hat and muddy makeup blotching his cheeks. The actor had his hand placed on his chin in a pensive fashion observing and nodding at his *oeuvre-d'art* with a content smirk. It was as if he knew this outrageous, scandalous, gruesome and offensive scene would gain him acceptance amongst London's theatre circles. He was like a rocket on the launchpad being pumped with fuel ready for his journey to the moon. Would he be the successful Saturn V or the exploding Soviet N-1?

Edmund turned to Holloway to seek his approval for the play. Holloway did not want to insult Edmund so he stuttered ambiguously. He expected the actor to see through his evasion and explode in a rage.

Edmund said in a mood turning from contentment to lecturing snark to childish glee, "I am glad to hear that you did not like it. Its purpose is to be a provocation. A provocation to people like you who cannot handle the consequences of their views. Here is the consequence of populist nationalism! A pure innocent world drenched in blood. You are all so priggish too so the fact that everyone is naked has not purpose except to be in tomorrow's *Daily Mail*! The performance is not just the 'acting' but also the reaction to it. The greater the backlash the better. This play, and many others, are not arts for arts sake but arts for the sake of provocation."

A miffed Holloway replied, "that's a bit shallow isn't it?"

"It's an honour to be attacked!"

Holloway had a different thought about the meaning of the final scene. The blood-soaked stage may contain actual blood, not red paint.

Meanwhile, in Tidworth's office, events were starting to take a turn for the worse again. Chakravarty and Hardy had both interviewed Martin Mansfield, the theatre manager, and had pictures of him throughout the office on various whiteboards. Tidworth believed he recognised him but wasn't quite sure, so he put out a call to some ex-army colleagues. The CCTV checks on Chamberlain Park produced nothing. The painter deftly positioned himself so that his back was always to the camera. The meeting Edmund was part of showed that he was present but not involved. It was quite clear that he was not the suspect.

Whilst heating up a microwave meal, a Tesco Chicken Tikka Masala, at about 18:00 with Tidworth's clock ticking very loudly, just 90 minutes before the premiere, Tidworth received a phone call from his ex-battalion commander about the picture. 'Martin

Mansfield' was in fact George Newark. He had served in 2 PARA during the late 1990s for a brief period. After finishing his dinner, Hardy checked some CCTV footage and found that Mansfield had been meeting the painter too in the park. It seemed he was certainly involved somehow in the theatre spy ring. But how?

"Oh Jesus! How did I not see this before?" grunted a frustrated Tidworth.

He went back to the kitchen area to fetch his curry.

At 19:00 in an office that now stunk of curry in addition to sweat and deodorant, Tidworth received another phone call from a senior contact in the Ministry of Defence. He moved the dirty plastic curry container out of the way whilst he answered his phone. According to the contact, George Newark served in 2 PARA from 1999-2001 before transferring to the Chemical, Biological, Radiation and Nuclear Regiment where he served until 2007. In 2007, he received a dishonourable discharge for hitting an officer. Since then, he had served various prison sentences for petty crimes. Tidworth was extremely concerned about Newark. Here was a potentially deadly man with knowledge of chemical and biological weapons – not to mention Major Sokolova and the mystery painter and gypsy.

At 19:05, with the office clock ticking louder, Tidworth strode out of his office in his greatcoat, leaving the plastic curry container out on his desk further polluting the office with its pungent pong, and threw down his gauntlet to his colleagues in the open plan area of the station.

"Right, I believe I have worked this one out. 'Mr Mansfield' or George Newark is going to kill Edmund and/or Captain Holloway with a chemical or biological substance. I am going to rush over there. Also, I am going to want backup. Get some armed police and a helicopter scrambled. It is going to be a really messy performance tonight."

"Err I thought the Superintendent told you to stay away and you were to have no support," interjected Hardy.

"This is the real deal! Tell her everything. We've got to go all in tonight."

Tidworth strode towards his Jaguar like a samurai warrior heading into battle. He knew exactly what he was doing and was in a state of zen when coupled with his car and his gun.

The journey to the West End was very difficult though. Tidworth swerved and sped through the busy streets of London. At times, he felt like he would lose control of his car and hid some pedestrians on the pavement. Buses and taxis were holding him up. Such a traffic situation was unusual in recent years, but on a Friday evening just as society was starting to restore a sense of normality, congestion was back. The lights of London were on, but there was an odd sense that people were keeping themselves to themselves more than before 2020. There was only one advert on the screen at Piccadilly Circus and it was British Airways advertising bargain holidays in the winter to the Caribbean. There were many people eating out at restaurants (particularly sitting outside under heaters wrapped up in big coats drinking hot chocolate) and going to the theatre. Nonetheless, there was enough space on the pavements for people to pass without bumping into each other.

From Piccadilly Circus, he was stuck behind a bus travelling at about 20 mph. Tidworth still didn't know exactly how the killing might take place. When he remembered his exchange with Edmund in the hangar a couple of days earlier. Punching his wheel, he exclaimed
"of course! It will be the Eau de Cologne. They aren't very creative are they. Just like Skripal all over again."

At 19:20, after being able to burn up the bus at a stop just before the theatre, Tidworth arrived at the back of the building and pushed through the door. He walked past a myriad of dressing rooms dotted with fairy lights. He frantically looked for Edmund's dressing room. At the end of the corridor was

Edmund Drummond-Moran's personal dressing room. Without hesitation, Tidworth kicked open the door to reveal an oblivious Edmund about to put his Eau de Cologne on. The detective ran towards Edmund and snatched the bottle out of his hand.

"What are *you* doing here?" said a perturbed Edmund wafting his hand over his nose at the smell of curry on Tidworth, "by the way, I really do think you need some of my Eau de Cologne. You smell like you have just had one of those awfully tacky and cheap microwaveable curries from Asda."

"Saving you from dying a horrible death from a nerve agent. You know that Mr Mansfield is in on the whole spy thing as well? He used to help the British Army with chemical and biological weapons. He knows what he is doing. This bottle is going to a lab and I bet you now you were seconds away from a horrible death. And by the way thespy boy, that curry was from Tesco!"

Edmund was starting to believe that his world was not actually real. His girlfriend and his closest colleague had been lying to him. Both were trying to kill him after framing and double-crossing him. It was like *It's a Wonderful Life* was playing out in Edmund life where the best action except that he would actually die at the end of the film.

Holloway scurried into the dressing room to see what happened. Tidworth was not pleased with his colleague's costume.

"I didn't think that green slime could have a downgrade, but it seems like it can," remarked Tidworth with a half-jokey, half-disappointed voice along with a smattering of military idioms that went over Edmund's head.

"I am undercover," he said with a muted grunt thanks to his mouthguard.

"Sorry. I couldn't hear you"

"I am undercover, what happened?" Holloway said with a crescendo after removing the mouthguard.

"Mansfield is GRU too. What's worse, he was in 2 PARA with me. Bloody traitor!"

"We are going on stage in about 5 minutes."

"Ok, I will deal with the backstabber myself. I'd turn the bastard into a Gregg's sausage roll if I could."

"Superintendent Watkins wouldn't approve of that."

"If I did the right paperwork, I might just about get away with it."

Holloway asked Edmund if he was still ok to perform after his brush with death.

"I must go out there and perform. My parents are watching the livestream on Zoom. Actually, we have a much bigger audience on there than those present tonight. My father, in particular, thinks I am an abject failure. Now is the time to prove them wrong. This is my big role. My pet project. It can't fail." The thought of failing his parents was making Edmund start to well up again.

Meanwhile, DCI Tidworth was trying to find his former army colleague, George Newark (aka 'Martin Mansfield'). He rushed into the foyer to find 'Mansfield' there.

"Have you had your temperature checked?" he asked the policeman.

"There is only one person that needs checking out here and that is you 'Mr Mansfield' or should I say George Newark, the dishonourably discharged soldier turned theatre manager," said Tidworth whilst pulling his gun on 'Mansfield's' head.

'Mansfield' let out a smug chuckle. "Oh yes, I remember you from 2 PARA. It seems as if you are a bit of a bigwig now. Why would you be so interested in a lowly theatre manager?"

DCI Tidworth brandished the bottle of Eau de Cologne that Edmund nearly used.

"What about this bottle of Eau de Cologne? A very effective way of dispatching people is by putting nerve agents in bottles of perfume. Who knows about Nerve Agents? You do!"

'Mansfield' clenched his jaw and just as he was doing that, froth started dripping out of his mouth that smelt of almond. Tidworth scrambled around helplessly and called backup into the foyer to deal with the dying man. He had taken a cyanide suicide pill. He was never going to talk.

As 'Mansfield' was dying in the foyer, the show was starting. The first scene was set in a *fin de siècle* living room. There was William Morris style wallpaper and two wing chairs with flowery patterns. Edmund was sat on one Sokolova on the other. They were both in period costume. Holloway was poised at the stage door with his pitchfork at the ready in case anything happened to Edmund during the performance. He could see that the audience itself looked a bit empty with one metre between households. The one thing that was perturbing Holloway was that he could hear the police reinforcements outside. Would that scare Sokolova into doing something rash?

The first scene comprised of Edmund's character telling Sokolova's character that he was signing up to fight in the army.
"What if you don't come back?" Sokolova's character said with a melancholy voice.
"I will find a way to come back," replied Edmund's character with confidence.
"Actually, you won't!" before she drew a pistol to his head. There was a deafening gasp in the crowd. Holloway was startled. He ran onto the stage and whacked her on the head with the pitchfork, dislodging the gun from her arm. She collapsed and Holloway kicked the gun away.
"Come on we have to get off stage now," Holloway said to Edmund whilst dragging the lead actor off the stage.
As they made their escape, there was a horrible 'whoosh' sound and Sokolova dropped dead.
"Jesus! There is a sniper in the gallery," exclaimed Holloway
As Holloway and Edmund went off stage, they bumped into Tidworth who was leading a group of armed policemen armed with flash grenades like a cavalry charge.
"We need to go up to the gallery now Len!"
"Ok!"
"Edmund, show me the way."

"Will do."

The three of them, tailed by armed police scrambled up to the gallery and found no traces of anything. Not even a bullet casing. "Damn! He has escaped. I bet it is the guy with the scar. We need to put out a call to all airports and ports to stop him from escaping," said a flustered Holloway

"Are you sure it was from here that he fired?" replied Tidworth Holloway and Tidworth pretended to aim as snipers from the gallery.

"Yes, the aim and angle seem about right," remarked Holloway.

Holloway, Tidworth and Edmund went outside to do a post-mortem of the situation. There were blue flashing lights, startled theatre goers and the sound of a helicopter hovering low over the theatre. Troops in white hazmat gear entered the building to examine Edmund's perfume.

"I think that we were close to ensnaring Major Sokolova," said Holloway.

"Were you? What was the plan?" said Tidworth in a quizzical way.

"To apprehend her in the interval."

"Really? As the perfume bottle showed, they were already onto Edmund."

"The problem is that we could have handled without this backup being so eager. It made the situation worse. She panicked."

"Ok," said Tidworth in a, weirdly, mellow voice with a sigh, "I will tell you a story of a lad I knew in Northern Ireland who was about your age. He went undercover in the IRA and gained their trust so much that he became part of their internal security unit. He knew everything. Then, one night, he said that he suspected he was in danger. We didn't send backup because we thought it might spook them. What happened? The next day, he was discovered in a river with a bullet in the back of his head." Tidworth now became much more self-assured, "I will not fail anyone undercover again! I will not apologise for doing what I did even if it was tactically wrong! I do not want another mate of mine ending up in a river with a bullet in the back of his head because I did not want to "spook" the enemy. I take full responsibility for what happened tonight. All of it and I don't care what some smug, smarmy, smart-arse fox-clubbing QC tells me in the inevitable inquiry. I won't let any of you lads down ever again!" before marching off and disappearing into the misty and dank autumn London night.

CHAPTER 6: AN OFFER NOT TO BE REFUSED

January 2024

In a large white cubed house in the Parisian suburb of Neuilly-sur-Seine lived a billionaire oligarch called Nikolai Travsky. He lived there with his wife of over thirty years, Alexandra, and his two children Alexey and Tatiana. Nikolai was a tall, thin man with fair hair and stubble. He always wore glasses. Behind these glasses lay a glare devoid of emotion that was so threatening he could persuade anyone to do anything for him. Nikolai was both intimidating and charismatic.

It was his aura that led to his heady success in the days after the fall of the Soviet Union. Travsky developed a cheap yet effective agricultural fertiliser to supply the vast agricultural regions of Russia – even helping crops to grow on the inhospitable and infertile tundra. His company was called *TravKom* and it was politically influential during the Yeltsin years.

In 1999, the inebriated and ailing President Yeltsin stepped down. The Russian economy was shot to pieces. His war in Chechnya had been a disaster. A barrel of oil was selling for less than $10. It was only unscrupulous and greedy businessmen like Nikolai who were coping with the economic situation. The man who replaced Yeltsin was a young and fresh former KGB officer called Vladimir Putin. He spoke German so he could appeal to the west and help foreign trade. Putin was younger and carried less baggage than older politicians. It seemed as if meaningful reform was on the way.

Nikolai courted this new president. The age difference between Nikolai and Putin was only about five years. Both originated from St Petersburg and had crossed paths when Putin was in the city's mayoral administration during the 1990s. From 2000, they met one on one twice a year.

In 2003, shockwaves ran through the Russian business community. The CEO of *Yukos* and one of Russia's wealthiest and most politically influential businessmen, Mikhail Khodorkovsky, was arrested for embezzlement and sent to a Siberian prison camp. The image of Khodorkovsky in a cage in a Siberian courtroom sent a powerful message to Russia's business community from the President. If you mess with me and try to play God, you will end up like a budgie in a cage.

Nikolai certainly played God. He was a popular TV personality and referred to himself as "the Tsar of fertilisers." From 2004, after Putin's re-election on the heel of a growing economy thanks to rising oil prices, Nikolai's access to the leadership began to dry up. He was frustrated that Putin's increasingly confrontational foreign policy with the west would damage his business.

In 2008, during the Russo-Georgian War, Nikolai made his first public move against the regime. In a public statement on television, he condemned Russian actions in South Ossetia and Abkhazia and called for an immediate ceasefire. The regime was angry. Fierce newspaper articles and diatribes on television erupted about Nikolai. His business associates were intimidated and attacked.

Now in open opposition to the regime, as seen by his prominent role in the 2011-2 protests across Russia, he ran for the presidency in 2012. When Nikolai turned up to a TV debate, a youth group associated with the regime assaulted him and then ransacked his townhouse in Moscow. Three hours after the end of the debate, he fled to Paris onboard his private jet. The vast majority of his assets in Russia were frozen and then expropriated. The "Tsar of Fertilisers" was left as a depleted refugee.

After some serious cost-cutting, he was able to buy shares in RB Leipzig, FC Sochaux and Sunderland AFC from 2013 but his wealth was never the same again. The private jet had to go. So did the Tuscan Villa. The Travsky family was left with a Parisian townhouse with a large staff and a fleet of seven Maybach saloons.

His opposition to Putin continued with him vocally condemning the intervention in Eastern Ukraine and the Skripal poisoning. In 2018, an attempt was made on his life in a restaurant in Paris. Glass powder was put in his dinner. Because it was not fine enough, he spotted it and the plot was foiled. Around the same time, shady figures repeatedly tried to gain access to his Parisian townhouse. Because of this security issue and the Coronavirus pandemic, he decided to build a new modernist style house in a forest west of the city near the River Seine.

In late 2023, a prominent Russian columnist and former Kremlin advisor, who went by the name of 'Roman Kozlov,' penned an 'investigation' into Nikolai's 'past crimes' in the government newspaper *Rossiyskaya Gazeta*. The piece detailed how he took government funds to grow *TravKom* in the 1990s and how, in fact, he used them to buy cars, helicopters and private jets. Nikolai knew this story was false and wanted to try and prove it wrong. He intended to sue the author for libel to try and regain some political standing in Russia. He said that he was to attend a court hearing on the 16th January in Moscow and he was going to travel on the 13th January Paris to Moscow express. Since the Coronavirus pandemic, Nikolai had gained an aversion to flying. Just before Christmas, he started receiving cryptic messages about someone threatening to kill him on the journey to Moscow. He worked out from one cryptic message that the assailant would have a scar down the left-hand side of his face.

Travsky had closely followed the details of the Yasnaya Polyana theatre group case. He knew Alexey Ostrovsky and Yevgeniya Tikhonova well since he had given them both safe passage from Russia. The lead officer involved in the case, DCI Len Tidworth, was now attached as a liaison officer to the *Police Judiciare* in Paris. There was a man with a scar down the left-hand side of his face who shot Yekaterina Sokolova dead at the opening night of the 'Cranes are Dying.' After several months of scouring from security services across western Europe, no-one could find a trace of him. On the evening of the 9th January, Nikolai invited Tidworth for talks at his house. It was a typically awful winter evening. Tidworth struggled to see whilst driving in his Jaguar up the lane to the property given the darkness exacerbated by the torrential rain. Tidworth swaggered into the hallway which had jet black reflective tiling and an atrium. From the ceiling hung a large circular chandelier, with a diameter equal to a king size bed, made of crystals. This room appealed to Tidworth's blingy tastes though he was taken aback by the strong ginseng scent that made Nikolai's house smell like a high-end retail store.

"Chief Inspector Tidworth, it is a pleasure to meet you," said Nikolai when greeting Tidworth, "my butler Kliment will take your coat." Kliment was Nikolai's loyal manservant. He had the stature of someone who had had far too many protein shakes with the dress of a *Downton Abbey* extra.
"Handshake," remarked Tidworth holding his hand out.
"Err, I think not," replied Nikolai in his monotonic yet fluent English.
"Oh, stop fussing. It has all blown over!" exclaimed Tidworth in a blasé voice.
"Shall we go to my boardroom."
"Of course."

'The boardroom' was a basement room in the house. It reminded Tidworth of a bunker. In the middle of the room was a large dark wood elliptical table, four television screens on each side of the room with an electric fire with pebbles on one wall. The room was lit with warm spotlights from above. Nikolai's favourite ginseng scent emanated from a reed diffuser in the middle of the table. Tidworth and Nikolai sat opposite each other on two tall thin chairs at the middle of the table. Given that this part of the table was the widest apart, they were probably two metres apart.

"I have been receiving death threats for several weeks now. I need your help to catch this man who will be on the Paris to Moscow express in a few days' time."

Tidworth looked rather puzzled at Nikolai across the table, "err aren't you going to end up like Navalny if you go back to Russia?"

"Possibly, but it could give me publicity if I get arrested. It is the train that is my main preoccupation."

"It isn't my job to control who the Russian authorities arrest in Russia. What happens to you on the train is a different issue. Unfortunately, I am quite busy at the minute with my own work in France. Finally, the police don't solve crimes that haven't happened yet."

"I have had to lay off my security because I don't have much money."

Tidworth grimaced at what Nikolai had just said. He thought about remarking that Nikolai should not waste his money on building a snazzy new mansion in the middle of a forest but he (just about, with much agony) restrained himself from speaking his mind for once.

"I know a couple of people in London who could help a lot."

"Who?"

"Captain Daniel Holloway. He left the regular Army in the Autumn and went into a reserve regiment about the same time I was posted over here. He might be free to do something. Captain Holloway assisted me on the Yasnaya Polyana case. I also know someone who met this man with the scar twice. He is an actor called Edmund Drummond-Moran. I imagine that as an actor he has plenty of time on his hands," replied DCI Tidworth, finishing off his answer with more than a little snark.

"This is very interesting. My daughter studies at the London School of Economics she can transfer the cash over to them."

"Not me?"

"You said you couldn't do the job."

Tidworth left the meeting with much chagrin at not getting any money.

The next day Tatiana Travskaya, contacted Holloway in London. They agreed to meet in Trafalgar Square where she would hand over the money. Holloway was quite pleased to be back in the action. He left the regular army due to the public nature of the fiasco surrounding the Yasnaya Polyana theatre incident in October. Alongside spending time transitioning to the reserves, he had worked for a Management Consultancy firm– ironically carrying out contracts for the Ministry of Defence. His two months work as a consultant was equivalent to an annual salary in the military. Yet, office life just wasn't as thrilling. The most mortal danger as a contractor was stoking the ire of a civil servant against a company who had a monopoly in the ministry's contracts.

Tatiana arrived at Trafalgar Square with a suitcase. Despite having a lecture on macro-economic theory immediately after her meeting with Holloway, she looked like she was dressed for a board meeting. As a graduate of Cheltenham Ladies College, Tatiana could well have sounded like a character from one of P.G. Wodehouse's novels. Holloway, on the other hand was dressed much less formally with his Barbour jacket and military scarf. If anything, he looked rather dishevelled and missing a purpose in life since leaving the regular military. Holloway needed a stopgap.

Tatiana outlined the details her father told Tidworth in Paris. She gave Holloway a suitcase of £60,000 to protect her father on his journey to Moscow and asked him if he could find Edmund. "I might have a bit of difficulty with finding him. I am able to be in Paris in two days so I will be very happy to do this."

"My father will arrange visas and the accommodation in Paris and Moscow along with the train."

"Wonderful."

"He used to have shares in Russian Railways and brought some luxury carriages for the express several years ago. We shall be travelling in them."

"Great, in the military we weren't particularly keen on frivolities so it will be good to at least travel in luxury."

Holloway tried to seek the unemployed Edmund out. A quick check with his old landlady in Bloomsbury confirmed he was renting a room above a trendy, hipster styled pub in Shoreditch. Holloway went up the stairs and knocked on the door. Edmund appeared looking exactly as he did when he was in the Yasnaya Polyana theatre group. This time he was wearing a tweed jacket, waistcoat and tie with his sleeves rolled up.

"Oh, hello, it is you again."

"You haven't changed much!"

Edmund and Daniel sat down on a dark red leather Chesterfield sofa. Edmund made Daniel a pot of green loose-leaf tea to share.

"So, what are you doing now?"

"I left the Army and worked in Management Consultancy for it bit."

"Worked?"

"I left it after about a month, and I am looking for stuff to do."

"So, it is as boring as it sounds. Never even considered it," responded Edmund with considerable pride at not having considered Management Consultancy.

"Absolutely. How about you?"

"Well, I have struggled to find acting jobs. I haven't even had an audition!"

"So…"

"I have been doing Great Fire of London tours dressed as Samuel Pepys."

Holloway tried to prevent himself from spitting out his tea

laughing. He obviously felt he had dodged a bullet with his dull Management Consultancy role.

Edmund reminisced about the theatre incident.
"So, that George Newark put Novichok in my Eau de Cologne."
"He did."
"I read some more about the Skripal poisoning. I would have died a horrible death if it wasn't for DCI Tidworth. I still don't like him as a person though."
"I think he is a complex man. The tough bravado exterior was peeled away to show a caring father-like figure. He is a man scarred by military action and absent friends. He was unflinchingly loyal to us even if he messed up the operation. I can't blame him for that. And what happened to *her*?" remarked Edmund with frustration.
"She failed," Holloway replied phlegmatically, "the GRU does not accept failure. There is a book by a former officer who goes by the name of 'Viktor Suvorov.' He described the organisation as like an Aquarium where the only fish are piranhas. In effect, Sokolova failed and was torn apart by the other piranhas."

Holloway then arrived at the question of the issue of providing security for Nikolai Travsky.
"I am currently looking for a job too and struggling. I don't have your ability to take the mickey out of myself so I could never do London ghost tours. However, I was contacted by Len Tidworth," Edmund did an over the top eye-roll when Holloway said that name. "He said that there is a Russian oligarch called Nikolai Travsky who is visiting Moscow this week and he is travelling there by train from Paris. Mr Travsky has received death threats from a man claiming to have a scar down the left-hand side of his face."
Edmund's eyes lit up.
"You mean he might be that man I met twice."
"Precisely. I have been given £60,000 to provide security for him on the journey. I need you to come with me to identify the assas-

sin. You know what he looks and sounds like."

"You want me to do a security job!" replied Edmund whilst almost falling of the sofa laughing.

"You get a 50% cut of £60,000 in cash!"

Edmund performed a *volte-face* quicker than any politician could.

"Well, yes, absolutely. It will pay for the rent."

"Deal?" said Daniel with his hand outstretched.

"Hand sanitiser?"

Edmund put some hand sanitiser on his and Daniel's hands and they shook on the deal.

"This man, if it is the guy with the scar, has destroyed both our careers," said Holloway with a sense of gravitas, "now is your chance and my chance to get back at him. This mission won't just pay your rent. It is revenge!"

CHAPTER 7 : TÊTE-À-TÊTE WITH NIKOLAI.

On the evening of the 12th January, yet another evening with torrential rain, Holloway arrived at the Neuilly-sur-Seine residence for his first meeting with Nikolai. Like the discussion between Nikolai Travsky and DCI Tidworth, it was held at the same oversized boardroom table in the basement of the white cubed mansion. Nikolai greeted Holloway in the same very matter of fact fashion he greeted Tidworth a couple of days earlier.

"You know my history Mr Holloway."

"I do."

"I know that my life is in danger. Who is sending the letters? Why are they sending them?" Holloway, for the first time, experienced Travsky's totally dispassionate manner in the face of clear mortal danger.

"What I find strange is that you are even receiving letters," replied Holloway whilst Nikolai looked very quizzical in his large chair.

"So, what can you ascertain from that?"

"The killer knows you well and maybe they don't actually want to kill you. They are giving you all these details to help you."

Holloway then asked Nikolai why he was actually bothering to travel to Russia. Nikolai answered that he believed he could restore his standing by destroying Kozlov's reputation. He admitted the odds were extremely low.

"From my time in the USSR, to the boom and bust of 1990s to Putinism, one thing stays constant in Russia. There is no such thing as "truth" and "justice." If you think there is, you are naive. Once you recognise that predicament, you become so cynical, even brutal. I wouldn't have been the man I was with the wonderful house, wonderful family and wonderful cars if I tried to be 'honest' and 'just.' However, I am the man I am now, running in fear of his life, because I tried to do the 'right' thing. I failed because I was just too much of an idealist and a dreamer. Now, I have to be brutal and destroy my enemies. Kozlov has been a waning figure for some years. Once upon a time he was Deputy Prime Minister then Deputy Chief of Staff to the President and now he is just a fantasist. Kozlov just pops up now and then to try and show the rest of us that he is influential."

Holloway then asked Nikolai more about the details of the operation.

"What exactly is my objective?"

"Do anything you can to stop me being killed on that train tomorrow."

"Even killing the assailant?"

"Mmhmm. Come with me," replied Nikolai whilst standing up and ushering Holloway out of the room with a bossy and patronising gesticulation.

Travsky took Holloway out of the boardroom to a different room in the basement. This time, it was just a blank room with a safe. What struck Holloway was how minimalist Travsky's house was despite the obvious expenses. It was 'in your face' yet bland. It had no personality except tasteless bling. Form, function and ownership all seemed to be one. Travsky opened up the safe and produced two handguns, Glock 17s, and some bullets. Holloway looked a bit startled.

"Why two?"

"One for you, one for your friend."

Holloway looked even more confused.

"I know I haven't been on the range for a bit but at least I can fire a gun. You expect him to fire one as well? You should categorically not be handing firearms to non-professionals. That's reckless."

"You will need all the help you can get. We both know we are up against some truly brutal and clever opponents. Your friend will have to use this moment to do something he has never done before. When you have been in such danger, as I have myself, you must adapt. He will be able to adapt. Trust me," replied Nikolai, staring at Holloway trying to get him to yield.

"I don't," said Holloway, standing his ground

"Take them both. When I was reserve officer in an infantry regiment just outside of Leningrad in the early 1980s, you never felt quite the same when you were without your gun," ordered Nikolai softly, yet raising his eyebrows in an intimidating fashion.

Holloway took the guns off Nikolai, who made a very astute point about the psychology of servicemen. Holloway knew that his gun was like his mistress. He slept with it all the time and when he cast it off after leaving the regular army, he felt like a void had been left in his life. Holloway made sure in his reply to Nikolai to heavily qualify his affirmation to cling onto an ounce of pride. "Right. Chekhov said that if there is a pistol hung on a wall and it doesn't fire in the next scene, then it shouldn't be there. By that logic, I will be using it pretty soon."

"Chekhov will be wrong!"

Holloway was getting worried that he had taken on a challenge that was too difficult for his ability. The man with the scar was an excellent enough marksman to shoot people from a distance. A skilled enough actor to hide his physical attributes when needed. Even though the scarred man was the main person of interest, did that mean he would be the actual perpetrator? Major Sokolova was an agent of his working in London. Surely there would be another Sokolova involved in the planned assassination of Nikolai. Holloway had no way of finding a wider network. Nonetheless, Nikolai Travsky was a strangely reassuring individual. His monotonic voice was calming and put Holloway somewhat at ease. He was dealing with an experienced and unfazed businessman who seemed to know exactly what he was doing. Holloway had no option but to trust Travsky's instincts.

Holloway and Edmund arranged to meet Tidworth for dinner later that evening at the George V Hotel restaurant at seven o'clock. Tidworth had put out a call to his French colleagues in the airports about a man coming from Russia with a scar on the left-hand side of his face. Holloway and Edmund arrived about five minutes ahead of schedule at 18:55. Tidworth turned up about twenty minutes later.

In their meeting at a large round table in the exquisite art deco restaurant with warm lighting and palm trees dotted around the room, Holloway asked Tidworth how he was finding Paris.

"How is it?"

"Torture."

"Well, that does surprise me."

"There is so much process and bureaucracy! Even more than there was in London. Oh, and I have to have an interpreter every-where. Right, nobody, I mean nobody, speaks English!" then pointing to Edmund, "and what on earth is that camp thesp doing here?"

"It is 2024, we do not use such language. I am not camp even though I did experiment a bit at Cambridge. By the way, I just want to thank you for what happened with the perfume bottle," replied Edmund with praise that sounded a quarter genuine, three-quarters sardonic.

"Just doing my job. However, my point still stands, what are YOU doing here? Oh, and I will use whatever language I like. Just like those people at the *Police Judiciare*," huffed Tidworth with a ham-fisted French pronunciation.

The dispute simmered a bit more.

Holloway looked at the menu and was horrified at the prices of some of the meals.

"This fillet steak is 50 Euros."

"It is the only steak in Paris that is not raw!" replied Tidworth.

"So, this is what our hard-earned money goes on?" said Edmund

in the fashion of a quizzing and morally superior headmaster.
"If you have any."
Holloway and Edmund looked at each other with startled faces.
Tidworth then launched into his life story,
"Listen, you two public schoolboys! Where I grew up in Stock-
port in a terraced house with four brothers it is like a cesspit,
right. The house next door to my Mum, there is a 14 year old
heroin addict. In the other house there is a 17 year old with three
kids. I grew up tight and saved and saved and saved so don't start
sniping at me for flashing around a little bit of cash when I have
a better job than both of you."

Holloway tried to mediate the dispute by ending it.
"Anyway, can we get back to the matter at hand. Have your calls
been successful? In answer to your earlier questions, Edmund is
here to identify the man with the scar on the left-hand side of
his face in the photos that you are going to show me now."
With a huff, Tidworth put the pictures on the table.
"A man fitting this description has been spotted on CCTV arriving from Belgrade at Paris Charles de Gaulle airport. As you
know when you arrive there, they film you having the temperature check as a record of your arrival and proof of health. It
seems as if he was travelling on a Serbian passport under the
name Josip Subasic and his original flight was from Moscow. His
health check form showed no Coronavirus symptoms. Thesp, is
this the guy?"
Edmund took a closer look at the photos.
"Yes, that is him. That scar is so recognisable," he remarked.
"The GRU are getting very sloppy indeed," said Tidworth snark-
ily.
Holloway cautioned Tidworth's smugness.
"Ok, we know it is him. But where is he in Paris? Who is working
with him? He is certainly not alone. Those letters will give us a
bearing. He had accomplices during the theatre operation."
"Aha, well, I can help you with one of those questions. Subasic
provided his address i.e. where he might have to stay in quar-

antine. It was an Airbnb near the Battle of Stalingrad Square. I told you they are sloppy. The GRU always provides you with addresses."

Their meals came and Tidworth and Edmund, in particular, kept on arguing. This time about food.

"You are not having steak! What a woos!"

"I am a pescatarian."

"What's that?" replied Tidworth who looked totally clueless.

"I do not eat meat, but I eat fish. The word comes from the Italian for fish," lectured Edmund.

"That sounds like the most pointless thing ever. All you can eat is fish and chips," said Tidworth with crossed arms leaning back in his chair.

"I can't eat Fish and Chips if they are cooked in beef dripping."

"What! That is the way they should always be done. What do you eat then? Leaves?"

"I eat healthily and ethically."

Holloway was looking totally drained at the Sisyphean arguments between Tidworth and Edmund. He was glad Tidworth was not travelling to Moscow. 40 hours in a confined space in the middle of a culture war would be insufferable! The next day was going to be very busy. He and Edmund were going to take a look at the Airbnb before travelling to meet the rest of the Travsky family. In the evening, they would travel on the train to Moscow.

CHAPTER 8: TRESPASSERS

The next morning, Edmund and Holloway set off to the Airbnb at Stalingrad Square. Since it was near a metro station, that was their means of transport. Public transport did not feel the same in the post-Coronavirus world. There usually would have been an eccentric jazz musician playing some 1950s Parisian café Chansons whilst begging for money. The trains would be so hot and sweaty with the sardines of people packed inside. The train was busy and bustling but not like it used to be. The world was the same, but more subdued.

Holloway and Edmund went down the steps from the raised metro station and found the street where the Airbnb was located. Edmund was wearing the same tweed jacket, waistcoat and tie from the day before and Holloway was wearing a black suit with no tie.

"So," said Holloway, "we want to have a look at that flat physically before we make a decision."

"What if he is in?"

"If we are dealing with an agent, he won't want to stay in one place for very long. He will be on the move. It is 10 am, he would have left by now, hopefully." as Holloway put Edmund's aviator sunglasses on.

"Do you think that it will be a huge risk with not much reward?" asked Edmund

"Coming from someone who dropped out of Cambridge to become an actor, that's quite rich. Now, remember your role here.

Look intimidating," replied Holloway sardonically to which Edmund huffed and shook his head.

They approached the typical turn of the century townhouse turned trendy residence and came to the landlady's reception.
"Good day," said Edmund in a very over the top Balkan accent, "my name is Slobodan, and this is my friend Alexander. We are from Belgrade in Serbia. I rang up earlier to enquire about one of your rooms."
"Yes, of course," replied the French landlady, "the last man who was here was from Serbia too. He left about an hour ago."
They went up an Art Nouveau staircase to the first floor of the townhouse.
The landlady pointed them to the first door on the right of the corridor and Edmund and Holloway went in.

The room was very light and airy. It had an oak-effect floor and white walls with abstract art on them. In other words, a white canvas with some sporadic splodges of red, blue and yellow paint. There was a room with a bed, desk and a balcony along with a kitchen and bathroom. The furniture all seemed very Scandinavian with light wood and functionality. Nonetheless, it looked a high enough quality not to have just been rustled up from a visit to *Ikea.* Unlike Nikolai Travsky's house, it seemed very understated and unfussy. However, there was a stench of alcoholic disinfectant that assaulted the nostrils of Holloway and Edmund.

With hushed tones Holloway outlined the plan.
"We need to be quiet. He might have left microphones and cameras. He probably knows if he provided his address that people will go looking for him."
"What do we need to find?"
"Hairs, fingerprints and any belongings. Don't forget the bins too."
The pair put on blue latex gloves and began their search.

Edmund checked the glass desk and chair. Both had been meticulously cleaned – so clean that he used the desk as a mirror to adjust his hair. Holloway checked the kitchen. Totally clean with the characteristic alcoholic disinfectant stench.

"It seems as if he has totally cleaned the place from top to bottom. Bins are empty. Everything. A true professional. We now need to check the toilet. I bet that has been cleaned too," remarked Holloway in frustration.

Holloway went into the Toilet and found one quite lightly coloured hair in the sink.

Holding it up with a pair of blue latex gloves, he said with a face of smug satisfaction, "bingo! This is the hair of the man who arrived at the airport isn't it?"

"It could be a wig? He was certainly wearing a wig when I met him when dressed as the gypsy. Although, I do believe that was his hair colour when I met him in the park."

"So, you think it is probably him Edmund?"

"Who else could it be? The landlady had black hair."

At 10:30 am, they assumed their disguise again as the two Serbians when they got back to the desk.

"Thank you so much," said 'Slobodan' to the landlady.

"You spent a long time in there. I am not sure what you were doing here but it all seemed very suspicious."

They scurried out of the front in fear of the fact that the landlady may have worked out what was going on. Edmund was breathing rather heavily and took off his aviator sunglasses.

"What do you think of that then?"

Holloway only seemed a little bit calmer.

"We gave away too much there, we needed to be more subtle. Now we must make our way over to Neuilly. I will get the hair off to Tidworth too."

The pair made a beeline for the Metro.

The taxi that they had caught from the nearby station had dropped them off at the end of the lane leading to Nikolai Travsky's house. This walk took about five minutes after they cleared the security gate. Despite the rain, Holloway and Edmund were sheltered by the trees lining the winding lane. The house was very well tucked away within the woods

"This is the first time you have visited Edmund," said Holloway to his companion as they turned up outside the white cubed mansion.

"Indeed but it is a little bit 'blingy' for my tastes. I prefer something more bohemian and cosier," said Edmund with a face that suggested he was a little unsure of what to make of his surroundings.

"Of course you do don't you!" replied Holloway with an eye roll.

They walked into the hallway where Nikolai greeted them both in his usually aloof and monotonic fashion. Edmund, despite scoffing at the architecture, really liked the ginseng scent in the entrance, sniffing with satisfaction. Nikolai, Edmund and Holloway then went into the living room. This room was certainly impressive. Because the first floor had been removed, it gave its occupants a feeling of space. Despite the floor-to ceiling window, the lack of sun meant that all the lights had to be on. There was a white extra-long curved sofa attached to the walls of the room. This room made the most of any light – if there was any.

"Mr Holloway and Mr Drummond-Moran, please meet my family."

First of all, there was Nikolai's wife, Alexandra. She was dressed in a black suit and was the First Deputy Chairwoman of *TravKom*. She had the aura of a fierce matriarch out of a Jane Austen novel with her short black hair and stern style with the fashion of a lawyer from *Suits*. Next was Alexey. He wore a turtleneck sweater, tight jeans and white trainers. He briefly took off his sunglasses and put down his MacBook to greet Edmund and Holloway before returning to his original position. His accent was very different to his sister's. Whilst Tatiana sounded like she could fit in on the Boxing Day Hunt, Alexey's voice sounded much more Eastern European with a slight American twang. Tatiana looked the same as she did in London – always overdressed for the occasion.

Sparks flew when the family started talking! Alexandra and Tatiana castigated Nikolai's excesses. They told him to sell some of his shares.

"The Sunderland Football Club is a huge drain on our finances," shouted Alexandra with a big pout.

"I am very attached to the players and the staff," replied a rattled Nikolai.

"We are spending and spending our money on things that just don't matter."

Nikolai then started firing – at his Son!

"Alexei Nikolayevich, you are a sponge, every kopeck I throw at you just seems to be absorbed. To what end? You just get bigger and bigger and do that stuff on your computer."

"Father, it is Cryptocurrency trading."

"There is no money in Bitcoin at the minute. If you even bothered to read any news you would know that!"

"I check it like every minute. You just read the *Financial Times* every month. Actually, I trade Ethereum now. Bitcoin is old! Don't you remember? Elon Musk trashed it." replied an irritated Alexey.

Edmund then joined in the dispute. He argued with Tatiana about her studying economics.

"So, you study economics, I remember those people at Cambridge. For them, an internship at Goldman Sachs was a substitute for personality."

"What did you study?" she said with a frown.

"English."

With a large cackle, she replied, "I would like a medium caramel latte with two shots please."

"Oh no, I had too much decorum to take up a job in Starbucks," he responded with a grimace.

"So, what did you do?"

"Acting."

"Useless. Just as I thought."

Edmund folded his arms and scowled at her.

Nikolai broke up the discussion and took Holloway and Edmund to his boardroom again. Nikolai sat at the head of the table whilst he was flanked by his two guests.

"I know it does not look good, but they are still a wonderful family. We are all travelling to Moscow together this evening. The reason why I brought you in here was to show you a video from a top television show in Russia last night. I wanted to see what you think of it. You don't need to understand the language. Just watch."

On one of the large flatscreen televisions, Nikolai played a Russian political talk show from the night before. The presenter walked into a studio that looked like it was set up for *Who Wants to be a Millionaire*. He began his shouty diatribe accompanied by dramatic film-trailer-like music. The floor had a screen showing an octopus graphic with the heads of figures like George Soros at the end of the tentacles. One of the tentacles had the head of Nikolai. The screen then cut to a group of masked soldiers doing military exercises. Nikolai's head then appeared in a gunsight and the soldiers fired showing fake blood dripping down his face. Edmund's mouth was wide open and his eyes almost coming out of their sockets. Holloway was shaking his head. Nikolai had his head in his hands before responding to the video.

"A slanderous and terrifying video. My Mother-in-Law was a Holocaust survivor from Minsk. How dare they! This is outrageous anti-Semitism! I am totally ashamed of my country. And our government lectures others on the Holocaust. Shame on them!" exclaimed Nikolai with the most emotion he had shown during Holloway's time with him – which was still not much at all.

"Are you still sure you want to travel tonight? That was an open death threat on that video. They did this to Litvinenko. I am not just worried about the journey; I am worried about what may happen to you in Russia."

"It must be done! It must be done! It must be done!" said Nikolai whilst tentatively banging his large table, "they try to use every little bit of bureaucracy to wear you down, break your character and if it fails then the violence comes. When that doesn't work, there is nothing left the Russian state can do. I repeat, if the Russian state cannot bureaucratically frustrate, injure or kill something, then it cannot defeat it. Plus, I have *some* allies in Moscow."

"Really?"

"I don't like to talk about them much. But when I arrive, at least I know not everyone over there will want to kill me," replied Nikolai so phlegmatically that Holloway thought it was an act.

Holloway was extremely concerned about Nikolai's safety despite his client's open confidence and defiance. He realised that there was no chance of convincing Nikolai otherwise. He had to sharpen his focus on the possible suspects. The Travskys were not such a 'wonderful family' after all. They were full of grievances and chips on their shoulders. Holloway observed the discussion from a distance and became despondent. All the family could be suspects.

Back at their Airbnb, Holloway and Edmund took stock of the discussion with the Travsky family. They were sitting in the kitchen diner which had a view of the Eiffel Tower, with the light on the *sommet* revolving around the night sky as if it was a lighthouse. Holloway and Edmund were sitting next to each other on stools which wobbled what they sat on them. They were made from metal that looked like it had come from a cotton mill in Lancashire and the wood seemed like darkened *Ikea* style chipboard. The kitchen itself was dimly lit with three vintage lightbulbs hanging from the ceiling onto the breakfast bar. Unfortunately, style and taste was prioritised at the cost of practicality. One had to stare at the food and drinks to see what it actually was. However, that tended to be par for the course for French interior design. Holloway listed his opinions on each member of the Travsky family.

"Alexandra: loyal to her husband. Desperately wants him to succeed and will do anything to make that happen – even if she doesn't exactly come across as warm."

"Well," Edmund responded with a voice that suggested he was going to contradict Holloway, "what if she believes she would be better at her husband's job?"

"Depends whether she has enough ambition. Next, Tatiana definitely sees herself as the future of the business."

Edmund grimaced at the mention of Tatiana as if he had just been eating some steak, "no, no, no. She was horrible to me about my studies."

"She wasn't wrong though. Anyway, Tatiana has clear ambition, but I am just not seeing a motive to kill her father."

"No-one liked his brother though."

"That's true. Not sure why you would anyway. The issue I am having with Alexey is that he just seems too sedentary to kill anyone. He doesn't seem to have the physical strength to pick up a gun."

"I can imagine him hacking his family's computers and discovering porn on them. You know that could be just as harmful as shooting one of his family."

Holloway turned his head round at Edmund, bit his lip and rolled his eyes for a couple of seconds to try and ruminate where the discussion could go after Edmund's rather sordid comment. All Holloway could say, with the dismissive and disdainful nature of a professor emeritus lecturing a failing student, was

"Erm, no. I don't think we should take the discussion there."

Edmund giggled intensely at what he viewed as his companion's Victorian, bourgeois, moralistic and priggish response. Holloway folded his arms, pouted and stared with disdain, at Edmund.

"Ok, ok," Holloway said whilst trying to move the conversation on, "we need to get dressed and put on a show tonight. We are in First Class!" Holloway's disgust shifted to excitement. Edmund skipped to his room to dress even more outlandishly for the journey like a child who was getting a train set for the first time.

CHAPTER 9: MISSION TO MOSCOW

It was 6 pm at the grand train shed of Paris's Gare de l'Est and the Paris to Moscow express was going to depart in 45 minutes. The darkness outside contrasted with the bright and bustling concourse on the inside. People were going home from work or going somewhere further afield. Many Parisians still smoked so there was a slight scent of tobacco in the crisp winter evening air. The Travsky family turned up at the station in their fleet of seven Maybach limousines. Two were to carry the Travsky family – the other five to carry various bags and Kliment. They were greeted by Holloway and Edmund on the platform. Holloway was sporting an Ushanka whilst Edmund was wearing a synthetic fur coat and a fedora. The scene of the express waiting to leave for the great cities of Berlin, Warsaw and Moscow was only missing some steam from one of the engines that traversed the continent in the time of the *Orient Express* and the *Train Bleu*. The dark blue carriages gave the train a feeling of luxury since they were the same colour of the *Compagnie Internationale des Wagons-Lits*, who operated these opulent palaces on wheels across the continent in the 1920s and 1930s. These first-class carriages were previously owned by and delightfully restored with the money of Nikolai Travsky. They were from the 1920s *Nord Express,* which travelled between Paris and Riga, so they were used to travelling the rails of western, central and eastern Europe. Everyone was dressed up for what seemed like a Live Action Roleplay of Inter-War Europe.

Before boarding the train, everyone had to have their temperature checked. Fortunately, everyone was fine. Holloway had positioned his cabin, number seven, which he shared with Edmund, in between Nikolai and Alexandra's cabin and their children's. Kliment was in cabin five. By being in the middle of the carriage, they could command the corridor easier. The end cabins, number four and number nine, had unknown occupants. The passengers went to their first-class cabins. They were panelled with lacquer wood with marquetry of the cities of Paris, Berlin, Warsaw, Minsk and Moscow throughout the rooms. On the right-hand side of the room, there was a sofa which folded down to form a single bed. Above, a wooden panel contained the top bunk. On the left side of the room, next to the window, was a separate seat so that the occupants could dine together face-to-face at a wooden table with an art-deco lamp. This side of the room also contained the door to the en-suite bathroom. It, like the room, was a luxurious affair. The walls were the same lacquered wood. The taps and the shower were all gold-plated.

Edmund remarked, "it is all a bit, you know, "Donald Trump" for me. You know that Russian golden showers did not go well with him?"

Holloway, who did not approve of his travelling companion's political views, said, "I am not going to have to put up with your bad lefty crude jokes for the next 40 hours or so am I?"

"They are simply accurate observations about our degenerate politics and society. They are not "bad" too. I honed my sense of humour at *Footlights*."

"Somewhere, in this carriage, is a cold-blooded killer, possibly our friend with the scar. We need to stay focused and on our toes. You might have a sense of humour honed at *Footlights*, but it counts for nothing against the GRU."

Edmund seemed taken aback at Holloway's *ad hominem* attack, "there is nothing wrong with a bit of a 'bad' lefty humour."

Holloway let out a big huff knowing that the argument could go on for the next forty hours, without a break if he didn't try to bring the issue back down to earth, and said, "right, the train is due to depart any minute now. We will need to get ready for dinner soon after."

At quarter to seven, the Paris to Moscow express lumbered out of the Gare de l'Est with a loud beep of the horn. It seemed like the train would never get up to speed by the way it creaked out of the terminus and into the grim *banlieues* of Paris. Heavy freight trains carrying everything from oil to cars to toys and commuter trains taking the ever-reducing number of workers in the city back to their homes seemed to be overtaking the sleeper train, whooshing past the window with their myriad of lights. Soon enough, the train cleared the rush-hour congestion of Paris and was on its way east towards the Alsace region and, eventually, the German border.

About an hour after departure, Edmund and Holloway went for dinner. This dinner was a black-tie dinner, very much an anomaly in the recent world. Thankfully, Holloway, who went to Sandhurst, and Edmund, who was an actor, were accustomed to dressing up. They put hand sanitiser on before heading to the dining coach.

"You can come up with the disguise this time Edmund in case we bump into someone who is not in the Travsky family," said Holloway.

"I don't know what I would do," replied Edmund.

"Who usually goes to Russia on a luxury train?"

"I have neither been to Russia nor been on a luxury train."

"Think, think, think. Be creative. You are an actor, you are supposed to be creative, aren't you?""

"I have just been doing Great Fire of London tours for the last few months. I just look stupid for busloads of tourists. I totally made a dog's breakfast of 'Slobodan' earlier," he said wistfully.

Holloway was starting to feel sorry for his companion after his initial frustration. He knew that his self-confidence had taken a hit since the theatre incident the October before. It still seemed like the Edmund 'of old' was there on the outside, but he was definitely psychologically different. His attempt at the 'Serb' was hammy and just not convincing. Holloway's attempt to summon Edmund's self-confidence was failing.

They strode along the corridor – which was punctuated by the very loud 'clickety-clack' of the wheels – towards the dining coach. Because of a newly fitted ventilation system, the air in the carriage had an ever so-slight chill to it. Nonetheless, the passengers were happy to put up with cooler air to avoid respiratory pathogens. This coach contained yet more exquisite marquetry and art-deco lighting. There were large armchairs at each table. Tables for four on one-side of the aisle, tables for two on the other. The first table for four had the Travsky family on it preparing to have dinner. Edmund and Holloway sat down at the second table for two in the carriage. The Belgian waiter handed them the menus whilst wearing white gloves and a white tuxedo. It was a four-course menu. The starter was either Melon or Foie Gras. The main courses were Fillet Steak with Béarnaise Sauce or a Goat's Cheese and Vegetable Tarte Tatin. The dessert was Chocolate Fondant. There would be a selection of French Cheeses followed by coffee. Holloway was pleased by the menu. Edmund was disgusted.

"There is no fish on the menu. This is an outrage. And Foie Gras! The year is 2024."

"We know it is 2024. You have told me many times before."

"But it is an unethical menu."

Holloway let out a frustrated sigh. Even without Tidworth, the journey to Moscow could be unbearable couped up with Edmund.

Then, two passengers came into the dining coach who neither Holloway nor Edmund recognised. They seemed like a couple. The man was about fifty and he had short hair with a black beard. He was definitely French and about six foot tall. The woman, who was either his wife or partner, had black curly hair and was a lot shorter than her husband. She spoke in an accent which sound a bit like it was from the north west of England. Interestingly, her and Alexey Travsky acknowledged each other sheepishly. They sat down at the table adjacent to Edmund and Holloway. The taller man introduced himself in excellent English, although it was recognisable that he was a French man fluent in English.

"Good evening, my name is Professor Jean-Christophe Masson, and this is my wife Bridget Masson," whilst introducing himself and his companion with a beaming smile on his face, "I regularly travel on this train and it such a wonderful experience. There is nowhere else in Europe you can travel in this luxury," whilst pointing at the cabin décor.

Holloway then had to think on his feet for a story. Meanwhile, Bridget appeared to be looking at Edmund. After some hesitation, Holloway cobbled together a disguise.

"My name is Benjamin Bowes and I am an oil trader with BP. I am travelling to Moscow on business with my associate here Edward."

Bridget was looking ever more inquisitively at Edmund, albeit with a slight smile on her face. Edmund knew that look. Somebody recognised him and was a fan. Unwisely, as a blatant tell of his guilt, he hid his face behind a menu.

"No, no, no," she said with a chuckle, "his name is not 'Edward' it is Edmund. He was in that episode of *Midsomer Murders* with the yoghurt factory. You remember that one don't you Jean-Christophe?"

"I do, I watch *Midsomer Murders* to learn English!"

Holloway let out his second forceful frustrated sigh in the space of a few minutes knowing that another one of his disguises had been foiled.

A quick conversation ensued as the starters came out.

"So, Mr Bowes, or whatever you are called, what are you doing on this train with the actor?" enquired Bridget.

"We are, well I am, providing security to one of the guests on the train. Edmund has some information that can help me. My name is Daniel Holloway"

"And who might you be providing security to?"

"Client confidentiality," replied Holloway with a smirk before asking about the couple on the other side of the aisle.

"I am Professor Masson. I am a police pathologist and a university professor. I will be delivering lectures at Moscow State University. I am travelling to Moscow with my wife, who is a teacher."

"Why the train?"

"I like the nostalgia and the contemplative experience of a slow journey after our previous life. Things were too fast so one did not have time to think about important questions. I have two days to think and to plan my lectures. This is excellent."

The meal passed and it was approaching ten o'clock. Whilst Edmund was not impressed with the menu, he at least did like the wines. Bridget too, who was a vegetarian, was not keen on the offer. Although, unlike Edmund, she was also a teetotaller. Holloway, on the other hand, very much enjoyed the meat focused menu. He had a couple of glasses of the Chablis with the steak and went back to his room and started to have one on ones with his fellow passengers.

The first conversation was with Alexey. He was a bit of a mystery to Holloway. Why was he so reclusive? Why was he doing Cryptocurrency trading? How did he know Bridget Masson? Holloway sat down at the sofa-bed side of his room whilst Alexey sat on the chair opposite. Thankfully, he wasn't wearing his sunglasses. Nonetheless, his aura was just as robotic and lethargic as it was earlier in the day with his neck and shoulders hunched over so much he was going to have a very sore back. Again, he was wearing his turtleneck sweater, tight denim jeans and white trainers whilst looking at his Apple MacBook. Alexey looked like he was making a hostage video.

"Could you put your laptop down please?" asked Holloway.

"Of course," said Alexey.

"And you do realise there was a dress code for the dinner," remarked an irked Holloway.

Alexey shrugged his shoulders in response.

Holloway began asking his questions, "so, your father told me that you do cryptocurrency trading on there."

"I do, yes."

"Why do you need to do it?"

"Because I am not the heir to the fortune."

Holloway seemed a bit startled and paused for a couple of seconds, "you are not going to inherit *TravKom* then?"

"No," replied Alexey curtly.

"Why?"

"The school I went to, the Neuilly-sur-Seine International School, they kicked me out."

"What did you do?"

"I took cocaine."

"Right," Holloway replied with raised eyebrows, "what were the circumstances surrounding you taking cocaine?"

"I just thought I would try it," he said with a shrug of his shoulders, "and my father saw me take it at a school concert."

"So, Nikolai reported you and you were expelled from a very good school. Then he cut you out of the considerable family fortune. How angry are you towards him?"

"Very, but I know he always preferred Tatiana. That was how things were always going to go. Therefore, I had to find other jobs to do," Alexey replied with another fatalistic shrug of his shoulders.

"Ah, interesting. There is one thing I am confused about. If you are very angry with your father and he is angry with you, why are you still living with them?"

"It is the best I can do. I don't live, I just exist and linger. Why not exist and linger around a nice house?" said Alexey with a phlegmatic chuckle.

Holloway was deeply unimpressed by Alexey at first. By the end of the conversation, he secretly admired his cynicism.

"One final question Alexey."
"Sure."
"Do you know someone called Bridget Masson?"
Alexey gave yet another shrug of his shoulders in response.
"Are you sure? You seemed to recognise each other?"
"No, it must be a mistake," Alexey replied with a shake of his head.
"You winked at each other. I saw it when she entered the dining coach," probed Holloway.
"No, I did not wink."
"You did."
"I didn't. You made a mistake. However, for a guy who drinks white wine with steak, what do you expect?" quipped Alexey whilst pointing his finger at Holloway.
Holloway was sitting back in his chair with his arms folded in frustration. Alexey Travsky was hiding something, and he just couldn't extract it from him. He tried a different method.
"If you don't answer the question now, I will tell your father that you are the person who is going to kill him. Also, I will have whatever wine I like with my food," Holloway said aggressively.
Alexey Travsky laughed at this insinuation.
"He probably thinks I want to kill him anyway! You think you can find out everything about me but, frankly speaking, you won't. Your detective skills are worse than your wine choices. You should just jump off this train!"
Holloway felt like nothing was going his way and he sent Alexey Travsky away. As he huffed and puffed back in his chair, Alexey threw a lifeline to Holloway whilst he was exiting the cabin door.
"By the way Mr Holloway, when you speak to Tatiana, ask her about the time she tried to sell her father's shares without his permission."
"Very interesting."
He concluded that Alexey was short of money with a dark history, so he was ripe for carrying out the possible murder of

Nikolai Travsky. Edmund had similar attributes, but it seemed that he was innocent. The difference was that Alexey was an extremely cynical person. As shown by his accusation of Tatiana, he would throw members of his own family under the bus to save himself.

Tatiana came into Holloway's room about five minutes later. This conversation seemed to go better than the one with Alexey. She gave succinct yet helpful answers to Holloway's questions.
"I think I should start with the most difficult question first. Why did you try to sell some of your father's shares last year?"
Tatiana began her reply with a nod.
"Yes I did. I tried to sell his shares in Sunderland Football Club."
"Seems a sensible idea," joked Holloway
Tatiana replied with a withering chuckle, "Yes indeed. I did not sell them because I wanted to destroy him but because I wanted him to succeed. The dividends were going to help us greatly. I do worry sometimes that his financial management is poor. After all, he studied agricultural engineering at university, not economics."
"How did he react to, what you could say, were your 'underhand' dealings?"
"He was not very happy with me, but we talked about it and he promised to improve his financial management."
"Has he?"
"Yes, I think so."
"You, 'think so?' What will you do if he doesn't improve his finances?"
"Well then that would be a big problem for me!" said Tatiana with a small laugh and a smile on her face.
"You probably know that your brother was originally going to inherit the fortune of *TravKom*. After his misdemeanours, however, you are going to inherit the fortune, aren't you?"
"I will."
"Did you father ever consider reprimanding you after trying to sell his shares?"

"No."

"Really? He didn't even consider disinheriting you?"

"No, Alexey will tell you that I am his favourite child. He is jealous but he is right. My father trusts me more than him. He spent all of his time at home. I spent most of my time at boarding school in England. I actually had to do things myself."

Holloway was satisfied with this interview. Tatiana gave short and relevant answers to his questions. Her body language was open, natural and relaxed. Alexey, on the other hand seemed very forced, up-tight and came across as a spoilt brat.

Alexandra was a handful. She was succinct – but maybe a bit *too* succinct with her answers – and intimidating.

"Good evening," said Holloway

"Good evening," replied Alexandra with a pout and walking in forcefully before sitting down opposite Holloway.

"I would like to talk about your family."

"I want water!" she said abruptly.

Holloway was a bit dumbfounded at the response and hesitated.

"I want water!" she ordered, again.

Holloway reached into his bag and found a bottle of Vittel he had brought in Paris. He put it on the table.

"I want it in a glass!"

Holloway was visibly flustered and wondering if this interview was even worth doing. He gave her one of the glasses provided in the room. As soon as she received the glass, she gestured bossily to Holloway to pour the water in.

"Are you ready to start?" asked Holloway tentatively after he had served Alexandra her water.

"Mmmhmm," she replied with a slow nod.

"So, I would like to talk about your family. What did you think of Alexey's drug use?"

"Very bad. He deserved to be thrown out of school."

"Did he deserve to be cut out of your husband's fortune?"

"Of course he was," she said with a look that suggested Holloway was dumb.

"Do you think he has a vendetta against your husband?"

"Yes, but he is weak, so it does not matter."

"Now onto your daughter. You know about how she tried to sell her father's shares."

"Mmmhmm."

"How did you respond?"

"I told my husband she did the right thing."

"Why?"

"My husband cannot control his money. He is a reckless man."

"Do you have concerns about his finances? Have you ever considered…"

"Watch your tone young man," she interrupted before storming out of the room and slamming the door shut. The glass of Vittel water Holloway tried so hard to provide for Alexandra to satisfy her discerning tastes remained untouched.

A few minutes later, Edmund arrived back at the room to see Holloway's head in his hands.

"Are you ok?" asked Edmund with a merry smile on his face

"No, Alexey is hiding something about his time at school…"

"Aha," interrupted Edmund, "I have just been talking to Bridget Masson and she used to teach Alexey Travsky."

"Damn it!" said Holloway banging his hand on the table, "so that was what he was hiding."

"What else happened?"

"Tatiana was ok but the mother. Wow! I thought she was going to rip my fingernails out."

"Well I have been enjoying the wine. They even had Chablis!"

"I can tell. Did you find anything else out from the Massons?"

"No, we mainly discussed theatre. Bridget used to be a drama teacher."

"I still don't know who is inside room number nine. This is so frustrating."

A drunk Edmund, with his bear, and a frustrated Holloway went to bed as the train was crossing the German border.

CHAPTER 10: OVER THE ODER

The next morning, as the train was nearing its next stop at Berlin, breakfast was served. The chef cooked up fresh omelettes with fillings on demand. The dining coach smelt of butter being fried along with mushrooms, ham, cheese, peppers and onions. Holloway had ham and cheese. Edmund had mushroom and cheese. The dress code was much less formal. Holloway was wearing an Oxford shirt to breakfast whilst Edmund was wearing a tweed jacket, sleeves rolled up, with an open-necked shirt. The Massons arrived at breakfast soon after and Holloway started talking to them across the aisle.

With a joyous boast and his usual big smile, the professor said that he and his wife were upgraded to first class just before boarding.

"It was such a surprise wasn't it, Bridget?"

"Oh yes it was," she replied with as much of a beaming smile as her husband.

Holloway enquired, "why and who gave you the upgrade?"

"The carriage attendant and the waiter in this carriage, Leclerc, gave us the upgrade. I believe it was some technical problem. When I used to fly, sometimes they would scan your ticket and it said you would be upgraded from Economy to Business class," said Professor Masson.

"If only that happened to me more," replied Holloway wistfully.

"Don't worry in Air France Business Class, it was just Economy with the middle seat blocked. They had nice wines though."

Holloway looked rather irked by Professor Masson's travel snobbery.

Leclerc, the Belgian waiter, brought over the Massons' omelettes and Holloway asked him about the nature of their upgrade.
"Mr Leclerc, my friends here are interested to know why they were so lucky last night!"
"It was a technical problem; my colleague scanned their ticket and it did not work. They were told to go over to me, and it worked. Plus, there were two spare cabins so there was space for them in cabin number four."
"Thank you very much. Could you tell me who is inside room number nine?"
"Unfortunately I can't sir."
"Was he upgraded?"
"I can't say sir."
"Ok,"

Holloway then asked Bridget Masson about her time as a teacher at the Neuilly-sur-Seine International School.
"So, my friend Edmund tells me that you were a teacher at the Neuilly-sur-Seine International School."
"Yes, I was."
"I was talking to Alexey Travsky last night, who was expelled from the school for taking cocaine. You two seemed to recognise each other yesterday evening. What is the history between you and him?"
"It is true that he was expelled for taking drugs. His father publicly goaded the school to expel him as a punishment. I stood up for Alexey and said that he deserved a second chance. He wasn't the *brightest* of pupils, but he wasn't badly behaved."
"When I asked him about the nature of your relations, he would not give me anything. Why do you think that is?"
"It was an incident that blackened my name and I was hounded out for standing up for what I believed in. It wasn't fair. I suppose he just wanted to make sure the story did not get around

further."

Holloway and Edmund went back to their room and discussed the situation.

"Ok I have a couple of jobs for you Edmund,"

"Right,"

"Look up Alexey Travsky's expulsion from school and it would be good to see what role Bridget Masson played in it. Also, take a look at her husband. I don't think we gleaned much from him. He seemed a nice guy but…"

"One may smile, and smile, and still be a villain."

"Exactly."

As the train left Berlin, Edmund's background checks produced some results.

"Ok, most of the details that Bridget Masson told us are corroborated by some newspaper articles about the expulsion. But, she is not actually called Bridget Masson."

"Oh really!"

"She is referred to as Bridget Jesson."

"She could have married since then?"

"Bridget kept a blog, which I must say I rather like, about the rehabilitation of drug addicts. Bridget cites her altercation with the international school and the Travsky family as her inspiration for getting involved in this cause. She is referred to as 'Bridget Jesson' in this blog too. However, there hasn't been much activity on it for a bit."

"And what about her husband/partner or whatever he is?"

"Well," he says with a smirk, "this is *very* interesting. Professor Masson turns out to be the regional secretary of 'The Flame and the Tricolour' party for the Île de France region."

"Oh god I can see where this is going. He is presumably going to Moscow for more than just a few lectures and seminars."

"Indeed. He seems to meet regularly with Russian ultra-nationalist politicians. He was in Moscow a couple of months ago meeting a prominent ultra-nationalist leader to declare 'War on

Islam' and that Istanbul should be reconquered and named Byzantium. It is so disgusting. He seemed such a nice guy when I met him!" Edmund said with wistful frustration, thumping his hand on the table.

"Well, you can't stop using that Hamlet quote about smiling and being a villain. We need to talk to them again. And please don't preach to Professor Masson about his political views. I don't like him, but we might need his cooperation – he is a police pathologist after all. Actually, *I* will talk to him and *you* can talk to Bridget! Oh and I am still not sure about the guy in room number nine."

Edmund and Holloway went back to the dining car after the departure from Berlin to talk to Professor Masson and Bridget Jesson. They spotted the Travsky family, minus Alexey, at one table. Bridget and the Professor came back into the carriage. Holloway and Edmund sat at one table facing the professor and Bridget, behind the table with the remaining Travskys.

Holloway was not happy with Professor Masson.
"Isn't it funny! You and your wife mocked me for going under a false name. It seems as if I am not the only liar here," Holloway said with a dash of aggravation.
"I don't know what you mean," replied the Professor with a chuckle.
"Are you married to Bridget Masson?"
"No,"
"You referred to her as Bridget Masson yet there are articles where she is referred to as Bridget Jesson. Why did you introduce her as Bridget Masson not Bridget Jesson?"
"Well, some unmarried couples have such an arrangement."
"Don't you think that, really, you are trying to cover for her."
The Professor seemed taken aback but still smiled.
"Mais, pourquoi! What has she done?"
"She got hounded out of the teaching profession for defending Alexey Travsky."

"Ok, ok, ok," replied the professor, clearly on the defensive, "I did not agree with her and she is a bit embarrassed about the incident so she decided to use 'Masson' as her surname to cover her tracks."

"How many lectures and seminars are you doing in Moscow?"

"Two. A lecture and then a seminar."

"Anything else?"

"No."

"Are you sure?"

"Sure."

"Ok then. What do you know about a political party called 'The Flame and the Tricolour?

Despite Holloway's pressure, the professor's usual smile did not move.

"Err yes I am the regional secretary for that party in the Île de France region."

"It seems as if you are regular visitor to Moscow too. You like meeting senior ultra-nationalist politicians. Your views seem to chime well with some of those at the top of the Russian state too," said Holloway whilst showing the professor pictures of his meetings with Russian politicians.

In response, he let out a big sigh.

"You have to believe me. You have to believe me. I might agree with *some* of what these people think but that does not mean I work for them."

"Like a war on Islam?"

"Take a look around the *banlieues* of Paris and you will agree with me! Furthermore, Macron has been saying that for the last few years. I am a political trailblazer. You are talking to a man who can influence the President of the Republic," he said with a smug smile, that grew as he outlined his perceived influence on French politics.

Edmund's conversation with Bridget appeared to a going a lot better – well, parts of it.

"What acting jobs do you have coming up?"

"Work is very dry at the minute. The pandemic really did hit our industry. Theatres had to be half-full or even empty. It was hard enough as it was! I was having some success recently and then the world seemed to collapse. Now I am having to do stupid jobs like ghost tours and advertising Marks and Spencer jumpers."

With a motherly aura, Bridget said, "Ahh, it must be so frustrating for you. I know it myself. You put in all those hours for auditions, rehearsals and then shows and you still don't know whether you will be able to pay the rent. That was one of the reasons I switched to teaching. Although look how that ended up!"

Edmund seemed to cheer up at Bridget's reassurance. He then moved to the question of Alexey Travsky.

"I just wanted to say how brave you were for standing up to his family and the school over him."

"Ahh, thank you very much."

"I read your blog too and it was so wonderfully written. I think that we should all have a second chance in our lives. How do you live with someone like that?" Edmund said pointing at the professor who looked round and acknowledged the statement with a wry smile. Holloway's worst fears had been confirmed and he put his head in his hands. Edmund was starting to preach and so the interviews fell apart. Little was gained out of this conversation with Bridget and the professor.

Sitting at one of the dining tables was a new passenger, who Holloway had not noticed before. The man had white combed back hair and a brutish scowling face. He was reading a copy of *Bild*. The man was wearing a pinstripe suit with no tie and his shirt unbuttoned two buttons. He was enjoying his cup of black coffee with the German tabloid and did not want to be disturbed. Since he had not met this passenger before, Holloway thought it was in his interest to talk to him. He moved over to the single seat opposite the new, probably German traveller, since he embarked at Berlin.

"Good morning, how are you?" Holloway said to this new passenger

"Ok," replied the passenger, who clearly did not want to be dragged away from his newspaper.

Holloway squinted slightly in puzzlement, "What is your name?"

"Dr Dirk Stirlitz."

"Daniel Holloway."

"What brings you to Moscow?"

"Tourism," replied Holloway with a shrug of the shoulders.

Stirlitz sat back in his chair, put his paper down and said, "tourists don't randomly sit opposite me on a train. I am usually being pestered by journalists wherever I go. I read slander every week about me in *Bild*," he whinged whilst pointing at the paper, "if you are a journalist, please go away."

"I am not a journalist."

"I am mystified by you, Holloway. I work in the gas industry. *Bild* is always saying I am a Russian agent because I work on Balt-Stream and I speak Russian. That's all you need to know about me," remarked Stirlitz in a curt manner. His tone then changed to an inquisitive one in the style of an interrogator getting close to extracting a confession, "what I know about you is that you are not a tourist and not a journalist. You didn't say you worked in energy. If you are travelling to Moscow, that means you are probably a government official or something like that. I am right about that?"

A humiliated Holloway stood up in shock and horror before walking back to the cabin with a sulking hunch where Edmund had returned with a post-breakfast coffee.

Holloway walked into the cabin with his mouth wide open before letting out a big breath when he sat down opposite Edmund at the cabin table.

"What has happened to you?" asked a concerned Edmund.

"I think my cover has been blown by that new German passenger," responded a panicked Holloway, "search him up, he is called Dr Dirk Stirlitz. You shouldn't have an issue with finding articles about him. Try and have a look if he is linked to Nikolai at all."

Edmund searched up on his phone for articles about the German passenger.

"Yes, I have found him, Dr Dirk Stirlitz, aged 66, Head of Governance at BaltStream AG, previously worked on the NordStream projects as a lobbyist."

"I have lost count of all the Russian gas pipelines. It seems to be all they do."

"BaltStream is a new pipeline proposed between the Kaliningrad and Rostock."

"Well that's three gas pipelines to Germany from Russia. What did he do before that though? What is his background?"

"He was served in various roles in the East German Interior Ministry before being appointed to the boards of many Russian banks and Russian subsidiaries of German companies."

Holloway shook his head in disappointment, grunted, huffed then whacked his fist on the table, "that first bit is basically code for 'he served in the Stasi.' It would just be my luck if he turned out to be our assassin. He will have strong links with Russian intel from the Cold War"

Edmund scrolled through more articles and found one that stood out particularly.

"This one from 2007 in Bloomberg talks about a clash between Nikolai Travsky and Dirk Stirlitz when he was Head of Global Governance on the first NordStream pipeline."

"Go on then," said an inquisitive Holloway, who perked up at the prospect of a tangible lead.

"Travsky wanted to invest in the pipeline. However, Stirlitz was told by the Russian government that Travsky was an undesirable person to invest in the project so he came away with nothing."

"So, it is more what Travsky has against Stirlitz that is problem rather than what Stirlitz has against Travsky. I suppose the pieces of evidence against him are that Stirlitz seems to have an intel background, he has links to the Russian government, and he knows Travsky is politically undesirable to Moscow. I don't want to talk to him again after last time but he is definitely worth keeping an eye on."

As the train neared the Polish border at the town of Frankfurt an der Oder, Edmund and Holloway went back to the dining coach and sat down at one of the tables to have another drink. Holloway asked Leclerc for a pot of tea with milk – to which Leclerc gave a subtly disgusted look. Amongst the passengers, Stirlitz had gone back to his cabin, so had Alexey Travsky. Holloway asked Nikolai where his son might be.

"He had breakfast and went back to his room," said Nikolai with his characteristically monotonic voice, "He is probably on his computer."

"Are you worried? Might it be a good idea to check on him?" a slightly agitated Holloway replied.

The rest of the Travsky family, Bridget, the professor, Holloway and Edmund went to Alexey's room. The door was closed but unlocked. Holloway opened it and everyone else peeped in behind him. They found Alexey dead, lying on the floor with a stab wound to the chest. Holloway, who had seen bloodshed before, Professor Masson, whose job it was to look at dead bodies, and Nikolai Travsky, who seemed to have few emotions, did not gasp in horror at the discovery of Alexey Travsky's body. Everyone else did.

As a police pathologist, Professor Masson was the perfect man for the moment. He had seen many stab wounds before.

"Ok, this job will be a little bit rushed, but I think I can work it out."

Everyone else left the cabin bar Holloway and Nikolai. The professor took a closer look at the chest wound.

"What is your hypothesis about the weapon?" asked Holloway.

"A very small knife. Possibly a scalpel. Ahh…" said a crestfallen Masson.

"What?" replied Holloway who dreaded what the professor was about to say.

"I brought a scalpel with me. I must check whether it is still in my bag."

The professor left the room in a hurry to check his bag. In his room, he furiously checked through his bag of medical instruments, breathing heavily. He emptied his bag onto the floor of the cabin. The scalpel was absent. Professor Masson came back to the murder scene flustered and his mood darkened.

"I am being set up!" he said with uncharacteristic anger, "they have taken it and used it to kill an innocent boy."

Masson, despite his anxiety at being a possible suspect, examined the body further.

"What do you think the time of death was?" asked Holloway.

"30 minutes. The wound is still extremely fresh," replied a shaking and flustered Masson.

"Well, I know exactly who has been out of sight for the last 30 minutes and could have broken into your room professor and this one. It is not you. It is Dirk Stirlitz."

Nikolai remarked in a deadpan way, "it seems as if no-one on this train likes me."

"It seems like somebody hates you a lot!" replied Holloway.

Meanwhile, Leclerc and Edmund came to the cabin with the steward carrying Holloway's pot of tea. The Belgian waiter looked as startled as everyone else did, almost dropping the tray.

"Where is Dirk Stirlitz staying? Is he in room nine?" Holloway demanded whilst pointing his finger at the waiter

"He is in the final coach, away from the dining coach. Cabin number three. Where should I put your tea?"

"That's the least of my worries. Edmund, Nikolai, we need to go to the next coach after I get some vital equipment," said Holloway, referring to his gun, with a rather flustered urgency.

After going to his room, Holloway, Edmund and Nikolai went to room three in the final coach. Holloway scurried off quickly ahead leaving the relatively unfit actor and oligarch behind. He banged on Stirlitz's door telling him to open up. The energy executive came to the door and make a rather phlegmatic remark as Holloway pointed his gun at him

"You know my English is not good as my German."

"You don't need to be a polyglot to understand what the barrel of a Glock 17 means."

"Well, you are certainly *not* a journalist."

"You are going to come with us to the dining coach to answer a lot of questions about the death of Alexey Travsky."

Stirlitz just caught a glimpse of his old business rival Nikolai Travsky.

"It is such a shame you could not invest in NordStream. We have built so many underwater pipelines since. Submerged pipelines really are becoming the future."

"Oh well, it would have been too much of a sunk cost," quipped Nikolai.

Holloway manhandled Stirlitz into the dining coach like he was a prisoner at a trial. The imagery of the dining coach was rather unfortunate since it was like a Moscow Show Trial of the 1930s. Like those Stalinist prosecutors, Holloway was convinced he knew the answer to the question. At a table, Holloway sat opposite Stirlitz whilst all the other passengers and Leclerc crowded round Stirlitz. There was great anticipation at what the results of this sparring match may be.

"Did you kill Alexey Travsky?" asked Holloway curtly.

"No, I was in my room the whole time," a calm and self-assured Stirlitz responded.

"You went from your room, you stole Professor Masson's scalpel and stabbed Alexey Travsky in the chest."

"There are several problems with your theory Holloway, whoever you are. Number one, who is Professor Masson? Number two, do I know where his cabin is? Number three, how would I know he has a scalpel?" argued an angry Stirlitz with his fists clenched.

"Because you are the mastermind of a plan to kill Nikolai Travsky."

Stirlitz let out a huge laugh, a laugh so huge it seemed like he was losing his breath and coughing.

"No, no, no!" said a stupefied Stirlitz shaking his head.

"Ok then, all the passengers are here. Which one is Professor Masson?"

Stirlitz pointed at the correct person.

Professor Masson nodded his head in shock. The audience gasped so much that it let like there was no air left in the carriage despite the improved ventilation

"See," said an utterly convinced Holloway, "I was correct."

"No! boomed Stirlitz, "it was a process of elimination. And question four, how did I gain access to Alexey Travsky's room? Question five, how did I know it was the correct room?"

"Because you were in the Stasi."

Stirlitz put on an even more stupefied face than before and replied, "what a lame and idiotic argument. Maybe I was wrong. Only someone with the low cognitive abilities of a journalist would conjure up something like that."

"No, I am not, I just left the Intelligence Corps of the British Army."

"Were you dishonourably discharged for incompetence?" probed a sarcastic Stirlitz.

"That doesn't exist," said a visibly irritated Holloway.

"They should have made an exception for you."

Holloway was frustrated that the ex-Stasi agent was starting to get under his skin and was diverting the conversation away from the main topic at hand. Holloway went back on the offensive at Stirlitz.

"Stirlitz! Which cabin is Professor Masson in?"

Stirlitz shook his head and shrugged his shoulders.

"Well say something then!" demanded Holloway.

"I don't know," replied Stirlitz.

"Don't tell me you don't know. You do know!" barked Holloway quickly sensing he was closing in on his target.

"Number four," said Stirlitz

The rest of the passengers and Leclerc breathed out massively as

Stirlitz answered correctly. Holloway kept digging since the suspicion that Stirlitz was the guilty party increased.

"Which room was Alexey Travsky in?"

"The same as his parents?"

"Which room was that?"

"Number five."

Holloway nodded his head and grimaced. He knew that Stirlitz was right. How could Stirlitz have committed the murder of Alexey Travsky with Professor Masson's scalpel if he didn't know which rooms they were in? Furthermore, Stirlitz was too flustered and under pressure at that point to concoct a credible excuse, so he was probably telling the truth.

"Ok, Mr Stirlitz you are off the hook for now. I suppose it will be trust but verify from now on."

"You have already had plenty of verification!"

Holloway decided to go back to Alexey's room to find a different answer. He noticed that Alexey's phone was on the side and it was still recording. He went back to the dining carriage, where most people seemed to be rather shaken, to ask the Travskys if they could sign into Alexey's phone. Holloway sat down at a table with the remaining Travskys. Tatiana knew the password and they listened back on the recording. There was a conversation between Alexey and another man from about 30 minutes ago that was getting quite heated. Holloway's translation (with the help of Nikolai and Tatiana) said that it went along the lines of.

"I just wanted the money and to wind him up, not to actually kill him," said a perturbed Alexey

The other person, whose voice had a gravelly croak to it, said, "I know the Englishman is onto you, he asked you some very tough questions."

"Viktor, he doesn't think I will kill him."

"That is what I expect you to do though."

"Well, I won't do it."

"I don't like people stabbing me in the back."

Then, there was a groan from Alexey as the assailant plunged the knife into his chest.

Nikolai with a sigh said, "so, he was betraying me. For the money!"

Alexandra joined in, "not only was he a waste of space, but he was working for the assailant."

Holloway chipped in to try and reassure them, "you know those death threats you were receiving Nikolai?"

"Yes," replied Nikolai.

"My theory is that Alexey sent those to you to help you out. Maybe this 'Viktor' found out that Alexey was double dealing. As the recording shows, Alexey just wanted some money and that was it. He thought that he wouldn't have to go through on his side of the bargain – although that was a huge risk to take. And at least we know Stirlitz is in the clear now, regretfully."

Notwithstanding, Nikolai and Alexandra did not seem too impressed with their son's conduct.

Edmund, on the same table as Bridget, had an expression that signalled he knew something.

"Could you play the recording again?" he asked Holloway

"Sure," replied Holloway.

After Holloway played the key extract, Edmund nodded and said, "aha, yes, that's him. That is the voice of the man I saw twice."

"For definite?"

"Yes, yes, yes, absolutely, it had that croak to it."

The one thing that concerned Holloway the most in the recording was the comment: "I know the Englishman is onto you, he asked you very tough questions." Holloway thought to himself, how did Viktor know this? Alexey could have told Viktor about the interrogation. Why was that not in the conversation though? Viktor raised Holloway and Alexey's conversation unprompted. That meant Viktor knew about the conversation before talking to Alexey. How could Viktor know about the conversation unprompted? Holloway's room was bugged.

A flustered Holloway asked Edmund to come with him to his room to look for any microphones. The two of them rushed along the corridors. Holloway wafted the door open after unlocking it.

Breathing heavily Holloway said, "Edmund, look in the bathroom, I will look in the room."
"What exactly do they look like?" asked Edmund.
"A small wire. I recommend using your phone torch. Look into cracks, look at mirrors, look at lights."
"Ok."
Holloway rummaged around almost every nook and cranny in his room. He ran his fingers down the sides of the sofa. When he got to the single chair, he felt again and was getting nervous.
"Edmund, have you found anything?" he shouted.
"No."
Then, Holloway's fingers touched a small wire down the crack in the side of the chair next to the window. Holding a small wire up at Edmund, who had just come out of the bathroom, Holloway said in a solemn tone.
"Viktor is onto us."

CHAPTER 11:
STRIKE TWO

Lunch was about to be served as the train was heading towards the Polish capital, Warsaw. The shock of the death of Alexey Travsky, though, put people off. Despite the exquisite lunch menu, most of the passengers opted for sandwiches. The train manager, Anton Grazin, a bearded man with a rather high pitched and strained voice came along the corridor to see if everyone was ok. Grazin, other than his rather high-pitched voice, seemed unassuming in his black suit, with decorated lapels, a golden button, and peaked Russian Railways cap.

"Hello," he said to Holloway and Edmund, "are you all ok after that?"

"Yes," replied Holloway sheepishly, "I have seen these things before but yes I am fine. By the way, could you tell me about the person in cabin number nine."

Grazin paused for a few seconds, and remarked impishly, "aha, yes, as you know, many eminent people travel on this train. Some of them just want a bit of privacy."

Holloway and Edmund discussed the Train Manager and the finding of the microphone in their room over lunch.

"Good to meet him for once. We haven't seen him at all on the journey. Just his voice announcing the stops," said Holloway.

"What do you think of the cabin number nine story?" asked Edmund.

"Hmm, it sounds like a VIP. Probably a government official. A senior spy?" Holloway responded whilst shrugging his shoulders as if to just throw a theory into the mix.

Edmund nodded in affirmation to accept that his travelling companion knew more about the matter than he did.

"How could somebody have got access to my room? I am sure that I locked it," said a confused Holloway.

"I don't know exactly who. But it could be somebody who has control over the train," replied Edmund.

Just as Edmund made his point, the Belgian waiter, Leclerc, came along the aisle to pour some coffee after the sandwiches.

"Mr Leclerc," asked Holloway, "do you know if there is CCTV footage on this train?"

"Unfortunately, sir, it is broken on this train," said the waiter

"Oh is it really? That is very helpful," replied Holloway with an eye roll.

"I am very sorry."

"No problem. Who could have access to our rooms? Somebody bugged mine."

"It depends when the bug was placed in there."

"Aha, so if someone placed it there, then they may have placed it at the beginning of the journey when all the doors were open. That widens the field a bit. Or, if it was placed there during the journey, then it could be..." says Holloway whilst looking round at Edmund.

Edmund put on an expression as if to display his innocence.

"You aren't suspecting *me* then?"

Holloway let out a huff.

"Well, I just don't know what to think. I just don't know. Whoever this person is has totally outwitted me. I just don't know where to start or where to look."

Edmund then went into soliloquy mode in response.

"Daniel, first you saved my life from a false existence in my relationship with 'Elena' or whatever she was called. Next, you saved my life from her in the theatre. Finally, you saved my life from mundane acting jobs. If there is anyone one this train who owes you, it is me!" Edmund leant forward in his chair as a show of trust. "If you ever find yourself in danger from anyone on this train, I want you to know, for certain, that I will be the first one to help. You are confused and you can't tell what is real and what is not. That is how I was last autumn. You can't trust anyone. I know the feeling myself. You need certainty and I am going to tell you this: I did not put that microphone in our room. There is only one person I am working for on this train and that is you!"

Holloway nodded along and could only muster a quiet "thank you" in response. Despite Edmund's persuasiveness, Holloway still did not know how the microphone ended up in his room.

Leaving the table across the aisle, Professor Masson returned to his room to work on some of his so-called 'papers.' Bridget started talking to Edmund about their various theatre roles.

"I fondly remember playing Ophelia with the Royal Shakespeare Company. I believe it was in 1992."

"I have played Hamlet," said Edmund with pride.

"Where was that?" enquired Bridget.

"Stroud. Only ten people turned up," he replied with a giggle.

"Aahhh, bless."

Holloway, who was not very well acquainted with theatre, felt very much on the periphery of the discussion. He remembered when looking through the bins at Edmund's flat that there was mention of 'The Cherry Orchard' in reference to the GRU operation that targeted the Yasnaya Polyana theatre group and, presumably, Nikolai Travsky. Holloway knew that it was a play but did not know the details of it. He used this point to enter the discussion.

"What do you two know about a play called 'The Cherry Orchard?'" asked Holloway with a bit of an ignorant look on face – much to the disgust of his travelling companions.

"That was one of my first roles!" replied a gleeful Edmund, "I was an extra!"

"Same!" said Bridget in a similar fashion.

"Ok, what is the premise of the play?" asked Holloway for the second time whilst trying to mask his frustration at the thespian travellers giving their life stories.

"It was written by Anton Chekhov at the beginning of the twentieth century. It details the life of the decline of an old noble family and the rise of a new middle-class family who used to be their serfs. The play ends with the 'cherry orchard,' owned by the noble family being chopped down by the ex-serfs," lectured Bridget.

Holloway was starting to get some threads from his thespian friends and came up with a few ideas. "I think Nikolai Travsky would be considered 'old' money – he is definitely connected with this whole operation. He made his fortune in a different time and is clearly in financial decline. The two theatre group members who were murdered were big stars quite a while ago but have been on the decline ever since they started opposing Putin. 'The Cherry Orchard' is about chopping down 'old' things."

Edmund then said, "it is considered to be a tragic farce."

Holloway let out an enigmatic chuckle. Nothing would be more tragic and farcical in his view than his outwardly amiable and loyal travelling companion stabbing him in the back all along. Before he could ruminate further, the professor entered the dining coach clutching his hand in pain. Bridget came up to him and tried to comfort him.

"What happened?"

"I have been electrocuted! I touched my door and it burnt my hand."

Holloway saw the deep burn marks on the professor's hand. He knew that this 'Viktor' person was still on the prowl somewhere on the train.

"Did you see anything or anyone?" questioned Holloway

"No. I went to read some of my papers. I finished it, opened my door, left my room, grabbed my door handle and I was electrocuted!"

Holloway went over to the professor's door but could not find any wires.

Shaking his head, he said, "nothing here." He became just as despondent as before.

One passenger who would presumably have some vital information was Travsky's manservant, Kliment. Holloway had not talked to him yet. He was obviously highly regarded by the family since he had his own first-class cabin. Holloway knocked on Kliment's cabin and the burly man dressed in his characteristic black three piece suit and tie ushered Holloway into his cabin. Kliment did not speak English so Holloway had to conduct the conversation in Russian. Holloway asked for the radio to be turned on to avoid bugs. There was a classical station on playing the Polonaise from Tchaikovsky's *Eugene Onegin* – very appropriate as the train was travelling through Poland.

"So, Kliment, I just wanted to ask about your relationship with the Travsky family," probed Holloway.

"I was first employed by *TravKom* as a security guard in the 1990s. I had just left the army. I served in Chechnya and I was one of the last Russian troops to leave Germany. None of us had a life after we left the military, so I am very grateful to Nikolai Travsky," replied Kliment with pride.

"So, you first worked as a security guard, what made you become so close and trusted by the Travsky family?"

"I helped them leave Russia in 2012 during the elections."

"That means you have been working for Nikolai Travsky for about 25 years and just under half of those years have been in the household."

"Correct."

"Therefore, when he started to lay off a lot of staff, he kept you on because of your loyalty and your skills in security."

"Correct."

"If you are their *de facto* security guard, why hire me?"

"I don't know, maybe he needs more people on the job."

"On Alexey Travsky, you were in your cabin when he was killed, weren't you?"

"Yes I was."

"Can anyone vouch for that?"

"No, unfortunately not."

Holloway was definitely perturbed by Kliment's lack of alibi. However, the fact that he owned up to it straight away did reduce Holloway's suspicion.

"What do you think of Alexey and Tatiana?"

"Alexey Nikolayevich was lazy and a drain on the family. He was totally useless. Tatiana Nikolayevna is the right one to take over *TravKom*. She has drive and she knows about business."

"Tatiana Nikolayevna tried to sell some of Nikolai Vladimirovich's shares and that got her into trouble didn't it?"

"Yes, but I intervened on her behalf and Nikolai Vladimirovich forgave her."

"Alexandra told me her it was her intervention kept Tatiana in line to inherit. Tatiana told me that her father did not even consider cutting her out of the fortune."

"I suppose she did intervene, but I really think that Tatiana Nikolayevna can make *TravKom* thrive in the future. I said this to Nikolai Vladimirovich"

Kliment was a curious individual. He was definitely loyal to the Travsky family. There was no question of that. He had a meteoric rise from a humble security guard to the family's sole manservant who was so valued that he travelled first class! There were discrepancies between Kliment's and Alexandra's statements though. Who had more influence in persuading Nikolai to keep Tatiana on: Alexandra, Kliment or Tatiana herself?

Before long, the train was pulling into Warsaw's central station. Leclerc informed the Polish police that there was a dead body on the train. The coroner and forensics team, dressed in white hazmat gear, put Alexey Travsky in a body bag and wheeled him off the train on a bed. Nikolai, Alexandra and Tatiana waved goodbye from the carriage door.

When Nikolai returned to the dining carriage, whilst the train was standing in Warsaw station, he asked Holloway for updates.

"Any leads Captain Holloway?"

"I have just been speaking to Kliment. He was in his room when Alexey was murdered so he doesn't have an alibi. Nonetheless, he owned up to that very quickly. Therefore, I don't think he is a suspect. Kliment also told me that the reason why Tatiana is still the heiress to *TravKom*, despite her trying to sell your shares, was due to his intervention, not Alexandra's."

"Very strange. I distinctly remember talking to Alexandra about the issue and it was definitely her intervention that changed my mind."

"So why did he lie to me? Did he lie at all? Was it just a misunderstanding?"

"I don't know. Anything else on Alexey?"

"No, unfortunately not. That is why I think you should get off here."

"But I have nowhere to stay in Warsaw."

"I think you will find that is the least of your problems. Your son has died. Someone else has nearly died. Surely you should call this trip off. It is too dangerous. You should apply the precautionary principle in a situation like this."

"Skin in the game," Nikolai replied with an unemotional stoicism.

"By the end of this trip, I think you will find that your skin will have been flayed!" responded an anxious Holloway who was visibly shaken at the fact Nikolai was willing to leave his dead son alone in Warsaw – aside from his client's utter recklessness.

"That may very well happen," said Nikolai with phlegmatic fatalism as the train started to lumber out of the bunker-like Warsaw central station and into the open air.

Holloway was dumbfounded. The person on the train with medical skills was partially incapacitated. Nikolai Travsky seemed to have almost sociopathic tendencies. Worse still, Holloway was beginning to have serious doubts about Edmund's loyalty. Who else could have put the microphone in his cabin? One may smile, and smile and be a villain.

CHAPTER 12:
THE MINSK
DISAGREEMENT

After the train's departure from Warsaw, the early night started to draw in over the snowy Polish plains. Holloway was in the empty dining coach ruminating over what to do next. He decided to give Tidworth a call.

"Hello," said a chipper Tidworth.

"Good evening," said a sullener Holloway.

"You got the lurgy from those russkies?"

"No. I'm stuck. How are you doing with the photos of that scar guy and that hair?"

"I should get an answer from London soon on the photos and the hair. What's happened on the train? Is it bad?"

"First, Alexey Travsky is dead."

"Jeez."

"Second, he was killed by a man who went by the name of 'Viktor.' Check that name out along with the hair and the photos."

"On it."

"Furthermore, one of the other passengers in our carriage, a French police pathologist called Professor Jean-Christophe Masson, who is also a prominent far-right French politician, was electrocuted today, only a few hours after Alexey Travsky's death. His partner, who uses her husband's surname, Bridget, used to be Alexey's teacher. Nikolai Travsky's wife is a total dragon. Then, there was a slippery ex-Stasi agent. Finally, there is a passenger in room number nine who is refusing to come out."

Tidworth chuckled a bit and said, "I should have skived off and joined you!"

"That would have been unbearable."

"How is the thesp?"

"I don't trust him. He bugged my room."

Tidworth, with a heavy dose of schadenfreude, chuckled even more and said "I *definitely* should have skived. I told you he was a bad egg."

"What do I about Edmund? What do I do about room number nine?" said a panicky Holloway.

"Confront Edmund. Confront the guy in room number nine."

"Bit over the top?"

"At least sort one of them out now. If it all goes to cock on the train, at least let it go to cock with the knowledge that you did everything to prevent it going that way."

Holloway made his mind up. Just before dinner, he would pretend to be the waiter, Leclerc, whilst knocking on the door of the mystery passenger. Holloway went up to room number nine and knocked on it.

"Bonsoir, it is Leclerc. What would you like for dinner?"

A tall African man with a beard and rimmed glasses came to the door.

"Yes."

Holloway was a bit startled, possibly expecting this mystery passenger to be a Russian spy.

"Who are you?" asked Holloway.

"Who are you?" quizzed the mystery passenger who seemed even more startled.

"I am one of your travelling companions, Daniel Holloway."

"I am Dr Goodfortune Joseph, a pleasure to meet you," he said after a breath of relief.

Holloway sat down at the table in the window of Dr Joseph's room and they started talking – with a classical music radio station on full blast. Holloway recognised that the piece was the fourth and final movement from Tchaikovsky's sixth and final symphony, performed days before the composer's untimely death.

"What is the reason for your journey Dr Joseph?"

"I work in the political affairs section of UNESCO. I am travelling to Russia to talk to the Foreign Ministry about the alleged discrimination of the Crimean Tatars."

"Alleged?"

"You read all sorts of russophobic things in the media these days. Have hope, forgiveness and solidarity," he proselytised with a smile.

"What is your connection to Nikolai Travsky or to the Travsky family?"

"I don't have one," replied Dr Joseph with a shrug of his shoulders

"Why haven't you left your cabin?"

"I have lots of work to prepare for my Moscow visit."

"To tell the Foreign Ministry that everything is fine?"

"You need time to be brief!" Dr Joseph said with an impish wink.

Just as Holloway started to leave the cabin, Dr Joseph mentioned something else.

"This cabin is really nice. I didn't expect to be in it," he said with a big smirk.

Holloway's eyes lit up.

"Aha, I know someone else who had an upgrade. How did you get yours?"

"It was a technical fault."

"Same for them."

"How interesting."

Because of this kernel of information, Holloway knew that Dr Joseph was yet another passenger with a connection to the Travskys. Why, like Bridget and Professor Masson, had he been put in the same carriage as the Travskys due to a 'technical fault?'

Dinner on the second evening was a more eastern European affair. The starters were dominated by dishes served with dill and mayonnaise. Beef Stroganoff was one of the main courses. The dress code was much more informal since it was smart casual. There was even an accordionist and singer singing traditional folk on the radio. The minor key songs seemed dreary and droning – which reflected the mood perfectly. The Travsky's table had one seat spare for their dead son. Holloway was sitting on his own having fallen out with Edmund over the suspected bugging. Dr Joseph too was alone in his room. Professor Masson was still in pain after his electrocution. Dr Stirlitz entered the coach and approached Holloway.
"You have a lonely job. So did I once."
Holloway nodded in agreement at Stirlitz's acknowledgement of his Stasi past. Holloway asked Stirlitz whether he was upgraded to first class as well.
"No, I choose this class all the time. Our company has very generous travel benefits," replied the German.
Stirlitz walked off to take a seat at his own table.

Soon after a quick passport and customs check by the Polish border authorities, the train crossed the border between Poland and the Union State of Russia and Belarus at Brest – the famous fortress city. The Belarusian border was over the River Bug. The Paris to Moscow Express trundled over the rusting metal girder bridge. The border was marked with two T-34 tanks on plinths illuminated in red and green lights next to an over-sized billboard showing Regent-President Nikolai Lukashenko and Vladimir Putin shaking hands. Underneath the two was a slogan in Russian which read, "happiness, friendship and brotherhood for the peoples of the Union State of the Republic of Belarus and the Russian Federation."

On arrival at Brest station, the bogies of the trains would be changed to the Russian gauge and everyone on the train would be given a swab test for Coronavirus. The Belarusian border was essentially the Russian border given the increased amount of Russo-Belarusian integration over the previous few years. The old and wily Belarusian dictator Alexander Lukashenko schemed and schemed to resist this integration, but he failed and ended up with a villa on the Black Sea Coast. His son, Nikolai, seen in the poster on the border, was, at the age of 19, essentially a puppet, manipulated by pro-Russian military and security figures whilst trying hard as his father did to resist further integration into Russia.

Brest station looked very bleak. There was snow on the ground. One could not see it well because of the poor lighting across the empty platforms. The only passenger train in the station was the Paris to Moscow Express. The other trains were oil and metal trains carrying said materials to western Europe. Everyone was led into the station building, a Soviet relic with WW2 music blaring out on loudspeakers. The passengers went through passport control to the Eurasian Economic Area which, as well as serving as a crossing for Belarus, allowed the passengers to avoid a passport check on the Russian border. The Coronavirus test waiting room was white and laboratory-like with black sofas. It had that recognisable stench of disinfectant, though it smelt even more lethal than the stuff that would be used in the west. In fact, Holloway's first reaction to the smell of it was a gag reflex. Holloway made sure he was in front of Dr Joseph in the queue for tests. A fierce-looking woman in a white coat and blue surgical mask with red hair that looked like it had been dyed with cheap chemicals marched up to Holloway and gave him his test kit first and told him to go to a room to take a swab – or rather gesticulated with a few grunts. In the room, he took a swab from his throat and a swab from each of his nostrils before going to a separate room where he waited for his results. This room just contained a large wooden table with wooden chairs around it with whitewashed walls. It was probably furniture out of a former local communist party office.

About 20 minutes after Holloway arrived in the room, Edmund walked in and sat opposite Holloway. For the first minute they just stared at each other across the table trying to work out what they were both thinking. Holloway started the awkward conversation off.

"So, we are alone in here, well there probably is a microphone, but it is a chance for you to come clean about, well, microphones," he said in a stop-start fashion and lacking confidence

Edmund stayed silent for a few seconds before constructing his answer.

"You have been with me for the few days since we met in London to discuss this trip. What opportunity did I have to plant the microphone in your cabin?" replied a perturbed Edmund

"We know that you had some contact with this 'Viktor' person we heard on the recording – the man with the scar. We only had your word on what your interactions were with him. So, I want to know *everything*, and I mean *everything*, about the nature of your contact with 'Viktor?'" probed Holloway, raising his voice and gaining confidence.

"He read my hand at the fair and said I would be successful. The rest of what he said was in Russian," responded a dumbfounded Edmund, wondering why he was being interrogated.

"True, the beaten-up gypsy confirmed that. How about the park meeting? You said the conversation was in Russian and you didn't say much at all. We only have CCTV footage to confirm the meeting took place. How did we know the discussion was in Russian rather than English – meaning that you could have taken part in it? Your word. You are an actor. I am an intel officer. We are both quite similar people. What do we do? We put on a performance, an act, a masquerade. I want people to have trust in me so they can divulge information. Throughout this whole affair, you have wanted to make myself and DCI Tidworth feel sorry for you. You came across as a pathetic, tragic and impish character. You made us smile, laugh at you and pity you. We did not feel revulsion towards you. I still pity you. Your talents are severely underrated. This character, whatever it is, is your *magnum opus* and I have been utterly convinced by it. So then, what did you discuss in the park?"

Edmund was breathing heavily and starting to sweat.

"Oh dear," Holloway said in a withering tone, "this is not looking good."

"I know," replied a flustered and desperate Edmund, "I should take my coat off. But, I *promise* you, I am innocent. What do you want me to do?"

Just as Edmund finished speaking, the dragon woman who gave Holloway his test came to give him his result.

"Eta nyegateeev!" she barked in the way a sergeant major would on the parade ground.

Holloway got up and said to Edmund.

"With the way you're sweating, I suppose we shan't see each other for a bit."

Edmund got out of his chair and went to the door to beg Holloway to listen.

"No, no, no. You are not thinking straight."

"What choice do I have?" before slamming the door in Edmund's face with the actor shouting at the door whilst banging it.

It seemed as if Edmund would be trapped in a Soviet-era theme park for quite a while.

Holloway ran back to the train to spring his plan into action to find out who Dr Goodfortune Joseph really was. The Paris to Moscow Express was still in the process of being disinfected by men in white suits with industrial electrostatic disinfection sprayers and a shunter going along the outside of the train spraying disinfectant on the carriages. Holloway was shocked that the disinfectant wasn't freezing in the air given that it was minus five degrees centigrade with crunchy snow on the ground. When he stepped back into his carriage, his gamble worked. All the doors to the cabins were unlocked for disinfection. He went into Dr Joseph's cabin and to look for evidence. It had a stench of disinfectant – that same nasty chemical smell that was inside the station. Rummaging through the top pocket of Dr Joseph's suitcase, Holloway found a business card for a management consultancy firm called Lagos Business Solutions. According to the business card, Dr Joseph was its CEO. Holloway had to be careful since he heard footsteps. He left the top pocket unzipped as he scurried out of room number nine.

Meanwhile Nikolai, who was the last person off the train at Brest, was having issues at passport control. His wife, daughter and manservant had gone ahead of him. Nikolai, like other Russian and Belarusian passengers, walked along the snow-covered platform under the white-backed and red-lettered sign for 'Eurasian Economic Area Citizens' and through a door into the room for passport checks. There was a white tiled floor and harsh white lighting that made his eyes twitch in bewilderment after coming in from the darkness outside. The queue for passport control zigzagged through an area that had the warmth and character of a hospital waiting room. A translucent barrier meant that it was difficult to see the passengers far in front. The line stopped and started intermittently as the border guards checked the travellers' passports. Nikolai felt it was like a game of snakes and ladders where there were more snakes than ladders. The queue seemed to move for fifteen seconds and stopped for a minute. Thankfully for the oligarch, he was able to reach the last square of the game. A translucent door that opened whenever the border guard pressed the button with the words 'passport control' above it in a red font. The only decoration on the door was what seemed like black plastic strips that formed a grid. One could mistake this shape for resembling the door of a prison cell or even the cage that Nikolai's former colleague Mikhail Khodorkovsky found himself trapped in Siberia 20 years ago.

At Nikolai's turn for the passport check, the plastic door flung open to reveal a Russian security guard at his desk behind a Perspex screen. A one-metre-wide channel led to a translucent door and eventually entry into the Eurasian Economic Area. He was wearing an over-sized black peaked cap and a blue surgical mask over his nose and mouth rendering it difficult to make out his age or facial expressions. The acne scars on his chin suggested the guard was possibly in his early twenties. On seeing Nikolai Travsky walking up to the desk, the guard inhaled heavily and raised his eyebrows.

"Is everything ok?" asked Nikolai dispassionately as he passed the passport to the guard.

The twenty-something opened the passport, flicked through the pages to the photo page to confirm his suspicions. The inexperienced guard flailed around his booth till he found his landline phone. He frantically dialled a number, possibly his superior, bashing the keys so fast he kept making mistakes. Nikolai stood motionless inside the translucent cage as the guard tried to seek help for his predicament.

"Colonel," the guard said in such a way that it was difficult to make out what he was saying, "Nikolai Travsky is trying to come back to Russia. What do I do?"

There was a break of about 30 seconds in which the "Colonel" responded to his rookie colleague. The response of the guard suggesting that the "Colonel" was in denial.

"Sir, it is Nikolai Travsky. You know *that* Nikolai Travsky they talk about all the time on TV. You have to see this," said the garbling guard.

The guard put the phone down, looked at Nikolai and told him his senior colleague was going to provide further advice on how to proceed. Nikolai nodded in response. Whilst waiting for the "Colonel," Nikolai stared at the guard behind his spectacles intermittently. The guard clasped his hands and tapped them on his booth desk like a metronome.

The cycle of Nikolai and the guard staring at each other lasted for around two minutes before the Colonel came into the translucent cage. The door swung open to reveal an almost obese man with clean shaven hair dressed in the uniform of the Russian Federal Security Service's Border Service. It was a dark green uniform with a dark green peaked cap. The buttons of the Colonel looked as if they were about to burst. He seemed to be a vainglorious and sarcastic man who enjoyed the power of controlling the borders at Brest station. Of course, it was an important task to prevent smuggling and illegal immigration into the Eurasian Economic Area. This Colonel seemed to rule Brest station as if it was the Russian Empire. Yet, there was a sense that a lot of his manner was simply an act.

"Nikolai Travsky, why did you come to Brest to die? Switzerland is a lot nicer," the Colonel blurted out with a large laugh.

"I thought I was here to cross the Russian border to attend a court case in Moscow," responded Nikolai curtly, whilst staring at the Colonel.

The Colonel smirked back at Nikolai and backtracked, "well, you don't get to own seven Maybachs without being a bit scary."

"That is the only clever joke, if that is what you can even call it, Russian TV pundits are able to say about me."

"You watch Channel One?"

"I am a very resilient man."

The Colonel led Nikolai to his cramped office. It was a rectangular room with a mahogany desk, an ergonomic black chair behind the computer with a wooden chair facing it. Reams of files on the floor of the office, overspilling from the already full cupboards, meant that actually accessing the desk was like trying to trample through a jungle. Behind the Colonel's desk was a portrait of President Putin from 2012. Next to the portrait of the President was a picture of the Colonel himself receiving an award from Putin in the Kremlin. On the adjacent wall was an ikon of the Tsar's family. After Nikolai and the Colonel sat down opposite each other at the desk, the border official explained his encounter with the President.

"In 2017, I received a letter, with the hand-written signature of Putin himself, inviting me to receive an award for my work as a border guard in the Kaliningrad Oblast." The Colonel rummaged through the pile of papers on his desk before bending over to look at the files on the floor.

Nikolai interrupted the Colonel's search for the President's letter. "This is the story you tell everyone you meet isn't it?"

"No, it isn't," replied the Colonel trying not to sound irked by the oligarch

"I used to meet Vladimir Vladimirovich every week when I worked in St Petersburg in the 1990s. When he became President, I met him probably about 20 times."

The Colonel straightened up quickly and stared with his mouth wide open at Nikolai then yelling like an envious child, "he doesn't like you much now though."

"Thank you very much sir, when I was nearly murdered with glass powder five years ago, I think I worked that out."

The Colonel stood up behind his desk, put his hands on the table, bent over and pouted at Travsky. He shouted, "I want to shoot you, Nikolai Vladimirovich."

"You will probably get another award from Vladimir Vladimirovich for that."

"I know."

"He may even give you his palace in Gelendzhik. Do you like aquadiscoes? I must confess I had never heard of one before. I was disappointed such a cultured man as Putin would lack that much taste."

The Colonel sat down again and put his head in his hands in despair.

"I hate you Nikolai Travsky, but I can't do anything without calling Moscow first."

"Go ahead."

The Colonel dialled a number in Moscow to ask for further advice on Nikolai Travsky crossing the Russian border.

When he got through to the contact in Moscow, the Colonel said, "Nikolai Travsky is here. Yes, I am sitting opposite him. What do I do?"

The contact in Moscow spoke so little that he probably only said a sentence. Whatever the official in Moscow said disheartened the Colonel greatly and he slammed the phone. He stamped Nikolai's passport as if he were having a tantrum. Nikolai took his passport from the dumbfounded Colonel and walked back to the train.

In the dining room, after the departure from Brest, Holloway and Nikolai discussed Lagos Business Solutions and Dr Goodfortune Joseph.

"What was your relationship with LBS and Dr Goodfortune Joseph?" asked Holloway

Nikolai nervously laughed. "That man, what an idiot. He supposedly had a PhD in economics from Oxford. I wanted him to restructure the African division of my business. He suggested bringing in these 'feel-good' people. At a meeting, he told senior managers in the company to eat 100% cocoa at a mental health workshop to help them achieve 'euphrenity.' LBS told us that we needed to have 'hope,' 'solidarity,' and 'forgiveness.' He said that I should copy his twitter page to improve my 'image.'"

"What was his twitter page like?"

"He would get thousands of retweets and likes for just tweeting 'hope' or 'justice.' And he thought this would help restructure my business? Shamans could have done a better job than him. The division was bloated, and it collapsed. I made sure that LBS was discredited."

"You destroyed his reputation in business then? How?"

"I did, I told all my African business contacts not to work with LBS. I called him a 'fraud.' I was going to write a column in the *Financial Times* where I was going to expose his witchcraft. He heard I was going to write the article and he dismantled his business in return for my silence. That is why he works for an international organisation. They are either failed politicians or failed businessmen. That is why they are all useless!"

Holloway chuckled at Nikolai's sanguine and cynical joke on the state of global politics.

"Well, you didn't just destroy his reputation, you destroyed his business and his livelihood Nikolai. That is a big grievance against you."

"He isn't doing too badly if UNESCO are paying him to travel first class."

"He wasn't originally. He was upgraded at Paris. Like the Massons."

"Hmm, very interesting."

"There is some sort of plan afoot to bring people who know you together. I just don't know who is masterminding it. Presumably, it is this 'Viktor' figure. Do you know *anybody* called Viktor in Russia?"

"There are many!" Nikolai chuckled. "Plus, how is your friend?"

Holloway sighed, "well, I think that he is on the whole plot too."

"Really?

"He put a microphone in my room."

"He did not."

"But who else could have? Who else could have had access to my room?"

"I am sure there is another explanation for it."

Nikolai went back to his room and Holloway had another drink in the dining coach. He decided to have a single malt whiskey. In between drinking it Holloway put his head in his hands on the table Whilst sitting at the table on his own, Tatiana came into the carriage and sat opposite him.

"Hey," she said in a warm and friendly manner.

"Evening," Holloway grunted back.

"You need waking up!"

Holloway looked at his watch and yawned, "I suppose it isn't too far off bedtime."

"Not at LSE it isn't!"

"University students, eh."

"Just completed an online lecture."

"Seems to be the way things are going now."

"I can be much more flexible with my time so I can devote more time to business activities."

"About that," Holloway asked whilst leaning back in the chair and starting to perk up, "I am very confused about why your father decided to keep you in the business. You suggested that he didn't even consider cutting you out. Your mother and father both said her influence saved the day. Kliment says his did. Who is right?"

"He never told me he was going to cut me out of the business," said a slightly startled Tatiana.

"Right," remarked a pensive Holloway, who was biting his lip, "because everybody else tells me that was his plan. Were you in Paris for these discussions?"

"No,"

"So, it was all done behind your back then? Well, that sounds familiar."

"In what way?"

"Everyone on this train is a liar. Everyone on this train has a secret. Everyone on this train that I have met is connected your father."

"I am really sorry if I have contributed to your confusion," replied an apologetic Tatiana.

"No, don't worry, you are far from the worst. The big question is 'Viktor.' Was Alexey his only accomplice? Is he still lurking amongst us? Or did he disembark at Warsaw or Brest? This is a game of cat and mouse where I am the mouse and he is the cat and I can't even see where or who exactly is the cat!" said a frustrated Holloway.

"I am sure you will protect my father from 'Viktor.' I shall leave you on guard."

Tatiana headed back to her parents' room with a hot chocolate.

About a couple of hours later, the train pulled into Minsk. This station was a desolate 1970s Soviet-era concrete affair. Still sitting in the dining coach, Holloway saw Joseph trying to run off the train with his various bags. To Holloway, this move seemed very suspicious. Why would Dr Joseph be running off the train? Was he in danger from someone? Was he in danger of being found out? The train would stop in Minsk for about 10 minutes. Holloway realised that he would have time to run after Dr Joseph. He chased after Dr Joseph across several platforms – nearly getting run over by a freight train in the process. This near accident hampered his progress. He saw that Joseph was getting away into the concourse of Minsk station. However, Holloway spotted an opportunity to stop Dr Joseph's escape. The floor was a totalitarian white marble. There was a cleaning bucket nearby full of water and disinfectant. This floor could easily become like an ice rink. Holloway chucked the contents of the bucket forward and Dr Joseph slipped over. Dr Joseph's fall gave Holloway enough time to apprehend the suspect, who was writhing around on the wet floor with the same slipperiness as an ice rink. He grabbed Dr Joseph and they went back to the train together.

In Dr Joseph's room, Holloway turned the radio to full volume (along with everything in the bathroom) to try and disrupt any possible bugs. The final movement of Tchaikovsky's final symphony – it seemed to be a popular choice at that very moment – seemed to do the trick again. Joseph thought that Holloway was behaving as if he was a bit insane. Holloway started some very shouty questioning.

"Why have you decided to hide away from everybody for the whole journey?"

"I told you, I have a lot of work to do."

"No you don't."

"I do."

"You told me you had no connection whatsoever to Nikolai Travsky."

"I don't."

Holloway held up the LBS business card. Dr Joseph laughed nervously and lost eye contact with Holloway. He knew his secret had been found out. But still, he kept on going with his original narrative.

"LBS did not work for Nikolai Travsky."

"Dr Joseph, you would be a rubbish poker player. That laugh sounded very guilty. I have talked to Nikolai Travsky about *TravKom's* relationship with LBS. He thinks that your solutions ruined the African division of his business. He took revenge by threatening to expose you as a fraud in the *Financial Times*. You backed down by dissolving LBS in return for him not writing the exposé."

Dr Joseph had been acting like the Japanese solider who did not surrender until 1974. For Holloway, it was so frustrating seeing somebody being so uncooperative. Now it looked like the tables were turning against Dr Joseph since he paused for about five seconds.

"Ok," said a hesitant Dr Joseph, "I saw that Nikolai Travsky was going to be on the train when his Maybachs turned up at the station in Paris. I can't even bear to look at that man after what he did to my business. I therefore requested to have all my meals in my cabin to hide away from him. My father was a teacher. We did not have much. We saved, we saved, and we saved. No frivolities. We went to church every Sunday. I went to college and then I won a place at Oxford. Nikolai Travsky will never tell you this, but he had all the privileges anyone could have had in the Soviet Union. His father was a senior party official in Leningrad. They had all the food and goods they could wish for. Caviar, cars and communism! He could go to university and get and do whatever he wanted. Yet, he thought he could play the moral high ground against me!" Dr Joseph, who had been very flippant for most of his time with Holloway now seemed to get emotional – and it was clear that he had a massive chip on his shoulder. His gesticulations and voice tone were a mixture of anger, wistfulness and envy.

"Thank you for that, I just thought I would enquire because there is credible evidence that Nikolai Travsky's life is in danger on this train."

"Why would I kill him if I can't even look at his face?"

"That is good to know. I think many of the passengers in this carriage have been set up."

Holloway decided to encamp himself in the dining carriage for the night. He didn't know if Edmund's test came back positive or negative, but he thought it safer to remain in the dining carriage, nonetheless.

CHAPTER 13: WIDE IS MY MOTHERLAND

It was two in the morning back in Paris. The water of the Canal Saint-Martin, just a few blocks away from the Gare de l'Est, was still since little traffic was passing through it. Most of the cafés and restaurants were closed for the night. The very faint light was provided by streetlights and the odd Metro train at Jaurès station. The air was wet. It wasn't quite cold enough for a frost, but one would need to wrap up warm. A trio of university students walked along the canal back from a massive night out. They all wore hoodies, adidas joggers, ripped at the bottom, with muddy adidas trainers. It seemed as if they were trying to dress as scruffily as possible. The scruffier their clothes, the higher their 'status' was. There was a man, about 20, in the middle of the group screaming incomprehensible sentences so loud that some people living in apartments turned their lights on to find out what the cacophony was. The female and male, about the same age, grabbed onto his arm to prevent him from swerving into the canal. Whilst swerving around the canal path, his blurred vision glimpsed what looked like a boot sticking out of the water.

"A boot, a boot!" he shouted in a blood-curdling fashion whilst pointing at the canal.

"You have had too many Jäger bombs," replied the girl in a dismissive fashion.

"Look a boot, a boot!" the drunk student shouted in the same way.

The two sober students looked round at the canal and saw at

the edge of the canal what was a mangled and smudge-covered corpse. They rang the police immediately. About 20 minutes later, along with some police divers and members of the *Police Judiciare*, DCI Tidworth arrived at the crime scene. He was already frustrated at being woken up in the middle of the night. The fact that he couldn't drive his car all the way to the scene turned his mood volcanic. Flanked by police divers with their suits on and many blue flashing lights on the road bridge over the canal, Tidworth swaggered down the steps to speak to the students.

"Right, can you lot tell me, in English, what the hell is going on here?" grunted the crusty DCI.

The drunk student shouted rabdily, in French, "the boot, the boot!"

Tidworth rolled his eyes and screamed even louder than student, "in Anglais I said!"

Just as the other students were about to respond, he received an email on his phone from the Metropolitan Police about forensics. It was labelled as urgent. He opened it up and the ordeal of the last few months started to make much more sense.

At 6 am local time, when the Paris-Moscow Express was firmly on Russian soil, the radio blurted out a song like a nursery rhyme. This woke up a bedraggled Holloway in the dark dining carriage. The sun showed no sign of rising outside. Then a female announcer said, with force, "attention, Moscow speaking," before reading out some of the main headlines. Vladimir Putin was going to receive some mothers who had given birth to ten children to give them a national award before having a meeting on Arctic economic development. Oil prices were still hovering at about $20 a barrel. Everything seemed perfectly normal.

Leclerc came along the corridor to switch the lights on and to offer Holloway some coffee and to ask for his breakfast order.

"Would you like some coffee sir?"

"Yes please. Black with sugar" croaked Holloway in response.

"Of course. How do you want your eggs?"

"I will have them scrambled this morning."

When the coffee and eggs came, Holloway told Leclerc to sit opposite him to discuss the mysterious upgrades.

"Mr Leclerc, there have been several passengers who received last minute upgrades to first class due to 'technical faults.' How often would you say you get these 'technical faults?'"

"They sometimes happen," replied the attendant with a shrug of his shoulders.

"Two upgrades on the same journey though? Isn't that quite rare?"

"Possibly."

"What is even more extraordinary is that all of the upgraded individuals had connections to the Travsky family. How do you explain that?"

"I don't know," said a sheepish Leclerc, who was physically backing off from Holloway.

"You do, don't you?" probed Holloway, who was starting to feel much happier now he felt Leclerc was on the ropes. "You have kept secrets very well before. Are you keeping one again?"

Leclerc scurried off to the kitchen. Holloway knew that Leclerc had been spooked by his questions. The waiter was definitely involved in the upgrades.

The other passengers came into the dining coach. Most people, it seemed, had tested negative for Coronavirus in Brest. Edmund did not come for breakfast. Holloway assumed that his sweating at the test centre in Brest was not just caused by him wearing too many layers.

Just after he finished eating his breakfast, Holloway received a call from Tidworth.

"I thought it was about four in the morning in Paris," remarked a shocked Holloway.

"Yeah it is, and I am blooming knackered," replied Tidworth.

"What's happened overnight in Paris?"

"Ok, we got an ID from London on 'Viktor.'"

"What did they have to say?"

"Ok, he is called Colonel Viktor Yegorovich Gerasimov, aged 43, married with one son. He is a senior officer in the GRU, ex-Spetsnaz and a veteran of many conflicts. He served in the Russo-Georgian War and Eastern Ukraine. We have also found evidence of him advising the Transnistrian government."

"Well, that is quite a surprise. A senior officer getting his hands dirty."

"You know I like getting my hands dirty too!"

"Maybe we should set up a meeting between you two. You might find a man after your own heart."

"No chance mate!"

"So, it is the man with the scar?"

"Yep."

"Isn't it a bit dangerous for an individual with a distinctive physical feature to be out on ops?"

"He obviously took the judgement that he would be safe."

"Gerasimov has been pretty professional so far – except going through Paris Charles de Gaulle airport. He must have left the UK illicitly."

"Yeah. There is something else I need to tell you. It explains why I am up now."

"Go on then."

"We have found a dead body in Paris in a canal near the Gare de l'Est."

"Right."

"It is a man called Anton Grazin. He is an employee of Russian Railways and was killed on the morning of the 13th January."

Whilst Tidworth was relaying this information over to Holloway, Dr Stirlitz dropped a note on Holloway's table as he went back to his room after an express breakfast consisting of just a coffee and pastry. It read 'Occam's Razor.' Holloway looked at this note in a confused fashion, squinting at it as if there was a cryptic code or anagram to be found from the two words. He knew what Occam's Razor was, but how could it be applied to the situation? Most interestingly, Stirlitz must have known more than

Holloway did.

"Sorry for the pause, I have just been reading something. You mean he was killed on the day my train departed to Moscow?"

"Correct."

"Do we know his occupation?"

"He was supposed to be the train manager."

"Aha…" said a Holloway confidently, grasping the meaning of Stirlitz's note, "I think I have worked it all out now."

"You sure this time?"

"Definitely sure. I met him yesterday! I thought he was playing a game of cat and mouse with me. It turns out that he was a cat amongst pigeons."

The call ended there.

Holloway realised that the whole case had been a farce all along. Gerasimov posed as the train manager, found passengers who were on the train with a connection to Nikolai Travsky and put them in the same carriage as him. That meant that Holloway's focus would be on the other passengers such as Professor Masson, Bridget Jesson, Dr Joseph and, in particular, Dr Stirlitz. Holloway could not have known who the train manager really was without knowing that the real one was dead. The train manager had control over the entire train. It was as if the passengers of the Paris to Moscow express were living inside a Panopticon. They were being watched but they could not see who they were being watched by. Gerasimov had sabotaged the CCTV to make Holloway's task even harder. Leclerc had been sworn to silence for the whole journey on the upgrades issue. He could enter rooms at the beginning of the journey, set the rooms up as he pleased and play passengers off each other. The bugging of Holloway's room was one such masterstroke by Gerasimov. He made Holloway distrust Edmund so much that Holloway would draw the wrong conclusions. The tragic farce was therefore not that Edmund was stabbing Holloway in the back, it was that Holloway had been tricked into thinking that it was the case. The mistake Gerasimov made onboard the train was trusting Alexey not to reveal details about his plans. The voice recording gave Holloway the best lead of the journey. Nonetheless, Gerasimov had succeeded in a *Maskirovka par excellence*.

Holloway knew that a tough fight would be ensuing with Gerasimov. His best hope was that a senior officer such as Gerasimov would be a bit rusty in hand-to-hand combat. Luckily, Holloway had the Glock 17 that Nikolai had given him in Paris. Holloway put on his coat, got up from his chair in the dining room and purposefully strode up out of the dining carriage into the sleeping carriage. From the door handle of Nikolai's room, Holloway saw a small wire running along the floor to a switchboard at the far end of the carriage. At the switchboard was the train manager with a scar down the left-hand side of his face after removing his fake beard. He wore a Russian Railways waistcoat and had combed-back fair hair – very much the colour that Holloway found in the flat in Paris. It seemed like there were endless amounts of gel in his hair.

"Good morning," said Holloway, in Russian.
"Don't worry, I speak English," replied the train manager whilst fiddling with the switchboard.
"Electrical fault? We seem to have had quite a few on this train. Did you hear about the man who got electrocuted yesterday?"
The train manager looked round at Holloway and said, with a menacing yet understated aura
"You know, Captain Holloway, it is very good to talk to you finally in my true identity. It will probably be a short conversation, but it will be a conversation worth having."
Gerasimov's insinuation that he was going to kill Holloway made him panic. He pulled his gun on Gerasimov. However, Holloway did exactly what the wily GRU Colonel expected him to do. Swiftly, Gerasimov yanked Holloway's right arm like a chiropractor and disarmed him. Holloway, in the corner of his eye, saw an axe to be used for fire escape He grasped the axe and took a swipe at Gerasimov's neck. As had been the case since

the start of the journey, if not the whole saga, Gerasimov was several steps ahead of Holloway. The Colonel ducked out of the way and Holloway missed on his swipe to the right. Holloway's swipe to the left was disastrous. He totally missed Gerasimov's body and the axe collided with the marquetry and became stuck there. Holloway had his back to Gerasimov and his head was lower than Gerasimov's. The Colonel pulled a gun to Holloway's head. Holloway had the dreadful feeling of the cold metal of Gerasimov's pistol and silencer on the back of his neck. He shut his eyes tightly in the expectation that he was going to be shot. He waited for the thud. Gerasimov did something very unexpected though. He pulled the emergency carriage brakes, thus stopping the train before leading Holloway out of the halted train into the western Russian wilderness.

Meanwhile, Edmund, who tested negative for Coronavirus in Brest in the end, glimpsed the horrific situation unfolding at the far end of the sleeping carriage just after waking up. It was shocking that Gerasimov didn't even spot him peeping through his compartment door given his outfit! That morning, Edmund seemed to be wearing his most outrageous clothes yet. He sported a blue velvet blazer, a colourful tie, a patterned shirt and chinos. He saw Gerasimov abduct Holloway and he ran into the dining room looking quite flustered. Edmund recognised the scar!

"He, Holloway, has been taken hostage. The murderer was the train manager. He was the man with the scar that was trying to kill you Nikolai," Edmund shouted into the dining coach, almost hyperventilating.
Nikolai shook his head in disbelief. "I have brought my old revolver. My Makarov. I used to be a Lieutenant in a reserve Soviet infantry regiment when I was a student in the early 1980s. Come on, we must hunt him down."
Edmund and Nikolai headed to their rooms to get dressed before heading out into the cold snowy dawn.

Tatiana then said, "my father is not very fit, he will need my help. Come on mother let's go."

Just as she was leaving with her daughter, Alexandra remarked. "This is like that book by Agatha Christie, Ten Little..."

"We call it 'And Then There Were None' over here," Bridget interrupted in a hectoring tone.

"Although, there was that person in the cabin that we never saw, along with us, so it should really be 'and then there were three,'" corrected the Professor.

"You are ALWAYS 'right' aren't you!" snapped Bridget.

Edmund and Nikolai stepped out of the train in their greatcoats and ready for their duel with the GRU. The scenery around the train was phenomenal. The sun was probably just about rising over the ancient birch forest, but the low cloud cover obscured it. It was that thick and dense cloud that one sees just before a snowstorm. It was a shame since there could have been a beautiful glare of the low and blinding sun accentuated by the snow-covered ground.

Inside the nearby birch forest, one could see a well camouflaged wooden church that looked like it pre-dated Peter the Great. This scene could have been copied and pasted from a novel by Pushkin or Tolstoy. Two intrepid travellers with traumatic backstories heading to a final showdown in a snowy Russian forest. Nikolai had his gun discretely stuffed away in his greatcoat whilst Edmund, very much detracting from the aura, was waving his around like a character out of a hammy American cop drama.

Holloway was led away to the church at gunpoint by Colonel Gerasimov. He was exhaling and sweating heavily wondering when exactly he would be shot. Surely the Colonel would pull the trigger sometime? Holloway's only hope against a skilful GRU Colonel, who had outwitted him for the last few months, was in the form of a sexagenarian oligarch and an unemployed actor.

CHAPTER 14: IN THE RUSSIAN CHURCH

Nikolai and Edmund were trying to trace the footsteps of Holloway and Gerasimov in the snow. It was very difficult to find out exactly where they had gone because there were many prints.

"He is going left towards the church," said Nikolai.

"No, he is going more to the right. They just seem to be heading to the forest," replied Edmund.

"No, my friend, they are the tracks of a local. You can tell from the footprints that Captain Holloway wears the shoes of a westerner. You can cover my back."

"Right, let's split. I will stay back and see if there is anyone else behind you."

"Do you know how to use one of these? You seem to be holding it like somebody out of one of those rubbish 1970s police dramas that I used to learn English from," said Nikolai pointing at Edmund's gun.

"Yes, I do actually. I was once in a play about a duel."

"So, I take it you don't actually know how to use a gun," quipped a withering Nikolai

"True, I was the one who got shot."

"Ok, I will help."

Nikolai partially stripped the gun to make sure the magazine was fully loaded and that all the parts were functioning properly. The oligarch's examination of the gun was very swift suggesting he knew very well what he was doing when it came to firearms.

"If you want to cock the gun so that you can fire it, pull the top part of it back, like this," Nikolai gesticulated. "I think for you, it is better if I put the safety catch on," said the oligarch phlegmatically whilst pulling a lever just above the trigger.

Edmund seemed a little bit overwhelmed and bewildered by the complexity of the weapon and the ease with which Nikolai seemed to master it. Nonetheless, after his crash course in weapons management, he took the gun from Nikolai and started to behave more sensibly with it.

Meanwhile, inside the church, Holloway was still startled that Gerasimov hadn't killed him yet. In fact, Gerasimov put his gun down on the floor and started talking to Holloway. Holloway wondered what was going on. He started chatting with his adversary of several months in the spartan interior of the Russian church. It was a dark tiled floor with wooden walls. The Church was cold enough to see condensation come out of their mouths whenever they spoke. The only ornaments in the church were some golden ikons on the altar, a forbidden place for the flock. There was a faint smell of incense.

"So, Captain Holloway, where did you serve?" said Gerasimov who seemed to be opening up in a disarming way.

"Well, I did a stint as an attaché at the British Embassy in Nur-Sultan a few years ago and I did tours of Cyprus and Estonia."

"Hmm, very interesting. I used to visit Tallinn a lot. A very nice city indeed. Its medieval walls are some of the best preserved in Europe."

"The GRU, I must say, have very cultured tastes. You really knew your facts about Salisbury Cathedral!" quipped Holloway anxiously, who now expected Gerasimov to explode with rage. Instead, Gerasimov let out a massive belly laugh and said, self-deprecatingly, "yes, that was not our finest hour."

Holloway did not know what Gerasimov's strategy was. Holloway initially thought that Gerasimov's amiability was a way of making him let off his guard and make unwise quips. But no. Gerasimov hadn't taken the bait yet.

Gerasimov opened up a bit more, "you know, I want to tell you a bit about why I am here, and I hope we can have a frank and open conversation about this."

Holloway decided to go along with this conversation. Gerasimov started first.

"I grew up in a city called Perm. Have you heard of it?"

"Yes, I have. It was significant in the arms industry."

"Correct. Both of my parents worked in this industry. What people who have never lived in Russia don't quite understand is that actually we did not mind the Soviet system so much. We did not like the, you know, excesses of it. However, it provided us with stability. Everyone had jobs. We felt like we could beat the Americans. Then, a group of politicians told us we had to forget this stability and that 'market forces' mattered more. We had to lick the boots of the IMF in Washington DC. We flayed our military to the bone. Less rockets. Less aircraft. Less tanks. My parents lost their jobs. We had to fight like dogs for the most basic materials. People like Nikolai Travsky became wealthy whilst the rest of us suffered. We could not buy the Maybachs, the private jets and the nice villa in Tuscany. We all had to suffer so that people like him could preen like peacocks. That is why I joined the military in the late 1990s. I felt that something was wrong with Russia. Frankly speaking, if you hate something so much, you have to actually do something to change it. I was not going to sit back in my dreary flat playing video games like the rest of my generation. And then, our chance came. One of our own came into power. I felt like I could make a difference for the first time in my life in Georgia, Ukraine and Moldova. I felt fulfilled. Nikolai Travsky fights for his Maybachs. I fight for Russia!"

Holloway had heard this spiel many times from Russians. However, Gerasimov put forward possibly the most effective and emotive case he had heard yet. It seemed very genuine and inspiring. Holloway then opened up on his life story. "When I was 18 or 19, I spent the winter of 2014/15 in Ukraine. It seems like we may have crossed paths before. I was volunteering at a school in the village of Debaltseve near Donetsk."

Gerasimov nodded in response.

Holloway continued, "I remember on Christmas Day, on the 7th January 2015 there was a service in a church like this one," and then pointing to one of the ikons in the church, "St Michael I believe. An RPG was fired at the church and it burnt down. 26 children who I saw nearly everyday were burnt alive. You seemed to know what I was talking about when I mentioned Debaltseve. I saw a picture of your colleague, Major Yekaterina Sokolova there. I thought that there was something rotten with state of the world. Therefore, I joined the military because of people like *you!*" shouted Holloway in the style of a prosecuting lawyer at The Hague.

Gerasimov still did not take the bait. Instead, he did something very different. The unflappable Colonel outlined a bold proposal, "you may be very angry. I understand. I felt like it myself. We are more similar than you think. We both look at the world and think what is wrong with it and how can *I* make a difference. I will tell you another personal story of grave injustice. During the Coronavirus pandemic in Russia, Nikolai Travsky sent a batch of ventilators to Russia to virtue signal." A tear ran down his scarred face. "My daughter, Nadezhda, you know what it means? It means hope. She had severe Asthma and caught Coronavirus in Moscow. One of his ventilators killed her. The people who made their billions unjustly lived off Champagne and caviar whilst the rest of us struggled to even buy cabbage and bread. The people who pontificated to us about how nice and liberal they were – and yet they killed our children! I am making you an offer. We can fix this injustice now. You can kill Nikolai Travsky. You probably feel betrayed by him, don't you? Don't worry you aren't the first person to feel that way."

Holloway curtly interrupted Gerasimov and raged, "you don't have a daughter. You have a son and he is still alive in Moscow probably living the life that you criticise others for having. I have seen the state of society in Russia. Hard working and thrifty Russians are queuing at this minute in Moscow, St Petersburg and a myriad of other cities to simply buy some cheap cabbage soup, bread and rags. And yet, their taxes are wasted on people like you gallivanting around Europe to re-enact a John le Carré novel. You framed a decent and innocent man, Edmund Drummond-Moran, because he was just cannon fodder. Yevgeniya Tikhonova and Alexey Ostrovsky? They were just cannon fodder, too weren't they? You killed an innocent teenager, Alexey Travsky, because he was a bit squeamish. Throughout these last few months, you have lied and deceived about myself and my colleagues. Played us off against each other. Made us hate each other. I would rather make a deal with devil than a charlatan Colonel from the GRU!"

Gerasimov was calm and collected. He knew which card to play next to induce Holloway to kill Nikolai Travsky. The Colonel nodded and remarked in a very matter of fact way, "yes, I very much understand why you might feel that way. You are quite right. I admit to what you accuse me of. I know it may be difficult to trust a person like me. But, when you have nowhere else to run, what other option do you have?" Gerasimov drew his gun on Holloway's head for the second time in about fifteen minutes.

The church door creaked open. The door was possibly several centuries old and poorly oiled. Gerasimov looked round and saw Nikolai Travsky come through the door pointing his Makarov pistol at Gerasimov.

"Aha, the crook and thief has come to save the day!" said Gerasimov with a snarky chuckle.

"It seems as if he has," replied Nikolai who pulled the trigger, hitting Gerasimov in the shoulder.

The Colonel let out a blood-curdling moan and fell onto the cold tiled floor. His gun fell out of his hand. Holloway picked it up and fired at close range to put Gerasimov out of his misery.

Holloway puffed as if a one-hundred-kilogram weight had just been lifted off his shoulders.

"You didn't need me in the end," joked Holloway.

"£30,000 for a nice cold holiday is not such a bad deal in my view," replied Nikolai.

"He was going to electrocute you. Professor Masson's electrocution was merely a test run. What a despicable man. He tried to feed me lies about his life. How he was a grieving father and that one of your ventilators killed his daughter during the Coronavirus pandemic," said Holloway.

"I never sent any ventilators to Russia."

"And he doesn't have a daughter. Then he tells me how he came from this city in the Ural Mountains and he felt he had to join the military because of 'burning injustices.' He tried to pit all of us on the train against each other. What a brilliant liar!"

"Mind you, we are all a bit like that really. Come to think of it though, he was an arrogant man. He should have just shot me there and then. He thought he could get me to kill you and wasted his time on something that was not going to happen. The GRU is like a metaphor for Russia at the moment. It looks very powerful and scary. It can act efficiently and brutally. But it is too outdated and sloppy to actually achieve anything," pronounced Holloway in the grandiose way Francis Fukuyama seemed to with his 1989 statement 'History has ended.'

"I think we need to get back on the train and hope it hasn't abandoned us."

"It might give us a chance to explore the countryside. I have only been to Moscow and St Petersburg so it would be good to do a bit of exploring and you could be my guide," responded Holloway in a dreamy fashion.

Holloway and Nikolai smiled at each as they began to head back to the train. As they walked towards the door, someone appeared there pointing a Glock pistol at them and said, "you have been duped!"

CHAPTER 15:
INTO THE FOREST
OF DEATH

The visitor turned out to be Tatiana Travskaya. She was accompanied by the Travskys' manservant Kliment and Alexandra, was being held at gunpoint and gagged by Kliment. The usually formidable and indomitable matriarch was reduced to a nervous wreck. Nikolai and Holloway stood completely still, not knowing what to do.

"Drop your weapons or she dies," ordered Tatiana.

"What is going on?" asked a startled Nikolai.

"I said drop your weapons!" screamed his daughter.

Holloway and Nikolai put their hands up and gave their guns to Tatiana, who emptied the magazines onto the church floor. The dropping bullets made a very loud 'ping' noise that echoed throughout the church.

"Outside! Now!" said Tatiana.

Holloway, Nikolai and Alexandra were marched out of the church towards some of the birch trees. The scene was a terrible beauty. A forest that seemed like it had been unblemished for centuries with a snowy floor. One could only hear the sound of foxes and eagles. And yet, it seemed as if this fairy-tale like snowy scene was going to be blood-spattered in a few minutes. They were lined up next to one of the trees. Kliment brought two large silver suitcases. He opened them up and constructed two black hunting rifles.

"Why do you want to kill your parents?" asked Holloway.

"I found out that Alexey had been recruited by the GRU to kill my father. I know how to sign into his phone and I saw WhatsApp messages between him and his handlers. I knew he would never actually do it. He just did it for the money. Then again, so am I! He is squandering my future," she raged with bitterness whilst pointing at her father. "When he dies, there is going to be nothing left for me, just a pile of furniture and paintings! I had to either sort out my father's finances, which he didn't let me do, or get rid of him. When you, Captain Holloway, came on the case I needed a contingency plan. If the GRU and Alexey failed, which they have, I would have to do it myself. Kliment has always helped me. He understood my predicament and that is why he is helping me!"

"So, you essentially made a pact with the GRU where you would let them kill your father by hiding the information from me."

"Correct."

"Why do you want to kill your mother? What has she done? She kept you in the family business when you tried to sell your father's shares. It was mostly because of her, not Kliment, that you will inherit the Travsky family fortune."

"She is just collateral damage. My father always says, doesn't he, that he wishes he was more cynical and brutal when he was in Russia. He blames his exile on the fact he wasn't willing to show some cynicism. I needed my mother as a hostage to make the operation work so, here we are. Actually, you made the situation worse by telling me that I was totally cut out of the discussions about my future. You have to understand, that is how it has been. I have just been a pawn," she said with her speech going from raw anger to pitiful sadness.

"Yes, but had it not been for her you would be like Alexey, just drifting. Now you are in line for a great fortune. You have your mother to thank for that."

"You know your history Captain Holloway. Bukharin, Zinoviev and Kamenev all helped Stalin get into power in some way or form – and look what happened to them!" Tatiana shouted, going back to her violent sociopath mood.

Holloway was quite terrified that Tatiana Travskaya appeared to be close to stealing Stalin's crown as Russian history's biggest sociopath. She was going to kill her helpful and loyal mother because she could.

"Ok, dear Tatiana Nikolayevna," begged Nikolai, "I can resign as CEO and Chairman now and you can be the CEO. You can be the brightest and richest young businesswoman in the whole of Europe. I know you can do it. Probably even better than me! That is why I made you the heiress to the fortune and why, despite your misdemeanours, I trusted you."

"I can resign as First Deputy Chairwoman too. You will make a better CEO than your brother would have done. We can retire and stay totally out of the business," suggested Alexandra in a friendly, maternal fashion.

She was not satisfied with their responses and laughed in their faces. "You are going stay in the shadows and treat me like some puppet, a Potemkin, token CEO. I know you so well."

Alexandra requested that she pray to God before her death. Nikolai joined in. They both made the sign of the cross. Tatiana looked unimpressed at what seemed to be such obvious obfuscation.

"Enough!" she shouted, as if to confirm Holloway's fears further about her sociopathy.

Kliment proceeded to put blindfolds on Tatiana's three victims and he bound them to some of the birch trees. Only Holloway, whose blindfold was the last to be put on, could see the glee in Tatiana's eyes when she felt she was on the cusp of gaining her father's business at no cost. Holloway tried one last heave.

"You think you are getting *TravKom* for free? You really aren't. The price you are paying is to have no family and to have on your conscience that you killed your mother and father. What if the authorities find out about you too? You may end up in prison for a very long time."

"They won't. We will shoot you. Then we will burn you. Then

we will pour acid on your bodies. Then we will put you all in a hole. Nobody will notice. People will dig your bodies up and find charred bones and they won't even know who you are. The nearest town, Sumasshedshayask, is forty kilometres away. I will go back to the train and say that the GRU killed you all and I tried to save you. And anyway, you say that losing my family is a big cost to me? It really isn't."

Holloway noticed some movement in the corner of his eye through the myriad of birch trees to his left. He did not know what it was at first. Then, a gunshot rang out and Kliment fell to the floor on his back with a bullet in his head. Holloway looked round and saw who the shooter was. Edmund had just shot Kliment in the head at a moderate range – which was pretty impressive given his lack of experience. Holloway had not seen his companion since Brest in Belarus and assumed he had tested positive for Coronavirus, so he was very pleased to see that Edmund was safe from Coronavirus and healthy enough to help out. The ordeal wasn't over yet though. Tatiana was outraged that Edmund sabotaged her execution at the last minute and turned her gun on him and she fired at him. Just after Edmund fired on Kliment and as Tatiana started to aim on him, he ducked so the bullet grazed his left arm and he shrieked in pain as he fell on the floor. Holloway knew that Tatiana would finish the job without fripperies or remorse. His friend had just saved him and the other prospective victims from imminent execution whilst putting himself right in the firing line of the unscrupulous Tatiana Travskaya. Now Holloway had to find some way to repay Edmund's fool-hardy favour.

Tatiana was within grasp of inheriting a multi-million-dollar business empire, improving it and enriching herself in the process. All she needed to do was to pull the trigger again and deliver the *coup de grâce* to Edmund.

When Kliment fell, he went on his back. That meant his pistol was easy to retrieve. Holloway had to pull out Kliment's pistol from its pocket and fire on Tatiana. She was prowling like a big cat to get closer and closer to the fallen and bleeding Edmund for the perfect shot. This move gave Holloway time to draw Kliment's gun and fire on Tatiana. Nonetheless, she had just about got to point blank range and was drawing her gun on Edmund as Holloway took Kliment's gun. Holloway fired on Tatiana as she was about to pull the trigger on Edmund. Holloway fired three rounds, at close range, and she fell. Such a sociopath could not be allowed any leeway. She had to be exorcised. Holloway immediately ran over to Edmund with Nikolai and Alexandra to deliver some emergency first aid. There was some blood on Edmund's dark green greatcoat, but mercifully not as much as Holloway feared. Holloway took off the coat to stop his blood flowing out. "Are you ok, has the bullet lodged in your arm?"

"Not too bad. It seems like has just grazed my arm. It has not gone in thankfully," croaked a clearly wounded Edmund in response. He was visibly grimacing at his gunshot wound.

Holloway took off Edmund's greatcoat and used it as a bandage to stop the bleeding. Nikolai and Holloway lifted him up off the snowy forest ground and they walked back to the train. Alexandra kept the pressure up on Edmund's arm to stop the bleeding. Nikolai held Edmund up from the other side of his body. It was a rather pitiful scene. On their way back to the train, they recounted what had just happened.

"Well," said a startled Holloway, "I have nearly been shot three times and I have had to shoot two people today." He took a big sigh, "people will come up to me and say that because I was in the military, it was an easy thing to do. Tidworth was right though. I was just a pen-pusher. I have shot at cardboard targets on a range. But not this. I have never had to shoot somebody. Colonel Gerasimov and Tatiana were awful people and definitely deserved to die, but…I don't know, it was harder than I thought. That is why, Edmund and Nikolai, I am so grateful for what you did. You aren't trained to kill, yet you rose to the challenge when you needed to – and it is not like being in a movie."

"If only!" joked a tentative Edmund.

"It is not a problem," said the monotonic Nikolai.

"Of course, I am very thankful for what you all did," chipped in Alexandra.

"It was a team effort indeed. Let's catch a train!" remarked Holloway

The four intrepid travellers walked back towards the train hoping it was still there. They staggered through the snowy terrain, crunching under their shoes. Edmund, whilst not seriously injured, would need some sort of assistance. The nearest town was quite some distance away. They had been gone nearly an hour. Would the Paris to Moscow express still be waiting?

CHAPTER 16: ALL ROADS LEAD TO MOSCOW

Holloway lifted Edmund up over his shoulder. The former crouched down before Edmund, grabbed the actor by hips and balanced him over his shoulder. The actor was between sixty and seventy kilograms so it was not easy for Holloway, who could feel the weight almost crushing his right shoulder. The best guide to finding the train again would be to follow Tatiana and Kliment's footsteps through the snow. Despite this aid, there was the underlying impression that Holloway, Edmund, Nikolai and Alexandra were in a very remote location. The only sound, besides the crunching of their footsteps, the squawks and the flapping of the wings of some birds of prey. If they fed on carrion, they would be in luck with four lost humans. When the travellers came nearer to the train, the surroundings started to become ever so slightly lighter. Their eyes twitched, adjusting to the light. The morning was murky, as if there was about to be another snowstorm, but the cover of the trees increased the murkiness further. The Church was the next milestone. Looking from the Church back towards the railway, one could make out the outline of the Paris to Moscow Express through the trees. Upon a closer observation, the warm lighting of the cabins and dining coach twinkled like seeing the harbour in the distance for the first time from a ship after an arduous journey on the cruel sea. Warmth, food and relaxation felt tantalisingly close.

The difficulty was getting on the train. Nikolai, Alexandra and Holloway had to lob Edmund onto the train – and hope that he didn't bleed too much. They lifted him off the floor and were ready to chuck him into the carriage. Leclerc came to the door just as Edmund landed on the floor so he could be lifted up.

"Don't worry, I made sure that the train stood still until you came back," said Leclerc.

"Thank you. We will need some alcohol for his wound. He has been shot," remarked Holloway with urgency.

Professor Masson treated Edmund whilst Holloway started talking to Nikolai and Alexandra at a different table.

"I am very sorry for your loss," said a solemn Holloway.

Nikolai paused for a second and replied, "it is ok. They both failed us."

"They both tried to kill us!" chipped in a dissatisfied Alexandra.

"I know," responded a startled Holloway, "but they are your own children?"

"It doesn't feel like it at the minute," said Nikolai.

"Ok, I will explain the full story of your attempted murder on this train by Colonel Viktor Gerasimov of the GRU. I think we know the situation concerning your daughter. At least four weeks ago, after the operation in London at the Yasnaya Polyana theatre group back in the autumn, the GRU were looking to eliminate more dissidents. Now, your son, Alexey, it seems, had been feeding details about you to Russian intel in return for money. They knew he was down and out, so they used him against you. When they heard about your visit to Moscow, they arranged for your murder on this train. Gerasimov was an experienced operative and he served across the former Soviet Union. He had to keep an eye on this operation. The London operation, which I had a role in foiling, did not go totally to plan since I exposed Major Sokolova. Yes, he succeeded in killing two of the theatre's main figures, but Edmund needed to die for the mission to be a success and he didn't. Gerasimov had to play a more active role in your assassination. He did not want to do it himself, but he made sure he was on the train in case he did. Therefore, he murdered the train manager, Anton Grazin, in order to disguise himself as the train manager. This meant that Gerasimov had access to all the rooms. He planted the bug in my room. He used the professor's scalpel to kill your son."

"But it did not go to plan."

"Exactly. I think you are being very harsh about your son. In fact, he was extremely helpful to me – and he paid for it with his life. As I said yesterday, he was feeding you details about the possible assassination to help you. Alexey simply felt like the operation was going too far so he tried to sabotage it. He hated you but he wouldn't kill you. We even knew what the assailant looked like and when the murder might occur thanks to his double dealing. Furthermore, he recorded his final conversation with Colonel Gerasimov thus allowing me to say for certain that he was on the train."

"But he betrayed me."

"He betrayed everyone. If he hadn't betrayed Gerasimov, he would have still been alive. The point I am making is that I think that he was a rogue and he behaved badly, but please, he is not comparable to Tatiana. He was killed because he did not want to kill you. And again, I want to say thank you to you. It was probably fitting that you killed Gerasimov in the end. Gerasimov, like he did with me, is excellent at pitting families and friends against each other so that everybody suspects those closest to them. He did the same with your family. But you delivered justice for your innocent son."

Nikolai, for the first time ever, looked like he was going to cry. The lifeless eyes behind his glasses started to go bloodshot and damp. He wiped them with a tissue. The iceman was starting to thaw.

"How do you feel about the court case and your security in Moscow?" asked Holloway

"Time will tell. They will want to humiliate me rather than kill me over there," replied Nikolai with a nonchalant shrug of his shoulders. It seemed like the thaw was a very brief interlude.

Alexandra then started to talk about her daughter.

"I am totally ashamed of her," she said with a justified bitterness as if she was swallowed a whole lemon.

"You are right," replied Holloway. "I just didn't see it coming at all. She seemed very cooperative with me at first. Alexey was the one who was hiding information from me."

"And Kliment too? I am just shocked at the fact he betrayed us too."

"My experience is that those who are closest to us and we think are least likely to betray us do end up doing so. I just wanted to pick up on something Tatiana said. I seem to remember she said "you say that losing my family is a big cost to me? It really isn't." I know all about the problems you had with Alexey but what do you think the problem was with her? From what I saw, you were both impressed by her commitment and drive. If anything, her problem was that she had too much of it. What do you say about what she said?"

Nikolai and Alexandra just shrugged their shoulders in response.

"So Nikolai, what is the plan when you get to Moscow?" asked Holloway.

"I have told my followers on social media that I will be arriving at the Belorussky Station and I will give a speech."

Holloway looked confused as to why Nikolai Travsky would expose himself to such publicity given his recent brush with death.

"Shouldn't you show a bit of restraint after what happened over the last few hours?"

"No."

"So, you want to be like Navalny then?" said Holloway with a muted chuckle, assuming the question was a joke.

"Yes."

Holloway stuttered a few unintelligible noises, trying to work out what to say in response.

"You have lied to me. There is no trial. That is just a ruse. You are literally going to Russia to get arrested?" responded Holloway eventually in a deflated mumble. He was disappointed that Nikolai had only revealed his true intentions so late in the journey and bemused at Nikolai's strategy to the point of struggling to speak. Maybe Gerasimov was half right after all?

"Correct."

Holloway stared at Nikolai, with his eyes wide open before flopping back in his chair in resignation.

"I suppose it isn't the first time I have been lied to in the last 48 hours."

"True."

"So why are you doing this?"

"Freedom."

Holloway huffed and grimaced at Nikolai with a confused look as if he had eaten a Heston Blumenthal Papaya Crème Brûlée with Lapsang Souchong Smoked Salmon. Holloway felt that people who deliberately intended to go to prison were either narcissists, nihilists or nincompoops.

"Err, you are going to prison. You realise that doesn't make you free."

"Wrong."

The crumpling on Holloway's forehead, in bewilderment at what he was hearing, intensified.

"I still don't follow. Why are you doing this?" Holloway stuttered once again.

"I didn't expect you to follow. You won't understand."

"I don't."

"Prison is the freest place I can be at the minute. I am free from everything. My business obligations. My possessions. Everything, you know. Also, they can't catch me in there."

"If 'they' refers to the secret services, then that's just delusional. In prison, they literally watch over you all the time. They control every part of your day. They can do anything they like to you. And that's not even talking about the other inmates."

Nikolai, paused, raised eyebrows and shook his head in response to Holloway.

"You see Captain, what you just described is exactly what has happened on this train. The GRU controlled all of us. They could hear and see everything we said and did. You mentioned the problems of other inmates. Look at what my daughter tried to do to. We were in prison. All of us. Our surroundings, luxurious, warm, and comfortable, gave us the illusion that we were free. And yet we weren't. It was all a lie. Where I am going, it is honest. It will be rough, cold and hard. I am making my own conscious choice here. I am the one in control, not them. I am the one who is sending myself to prison, not them. What I am doing is the ultimate expression of true and honest free will."

Holloway stared at Nikolai in response. He ruminated for a few seconds, trying to find a response.

"Did I just hear a GCSE Philosophy essay?" he said.

"That is the difference between us and the British. You are just so superficial. Loyal and brave but psychologically and spiritually superficial. You are a very good representation of that Captain Holloway. Take it as a compliment" responded the oligarch with a slight irritation.

"Does your wife know about this?"

"Of course. She will be joining me. But seriously, I am sorry if I have confused or insulted you. Captain Holloway, and not to mention your friend, you have shown exceptional bravery. You have delivered me safely to Moscow. I could not die at the hands of Colonel Gerasimov. If I am to die, it will be my own choice, and mine only. You too have liberated me. Now, I must begin the next stage of my journey."

Nikolai and Alexandra headed back to their rooms to sort out their belongings. Holloway judged that Nikolai was being sincere this time. Why would a man who was just about to spend time in the frigid psychological and physical bear pit that was the Russian penitentiary system be acting so normally? The same went for his wife, though she appeared to have little input on the matter. Nikolai just seemed to expect that she would join him in his act of nihilism in the name of 'true and honest free will.'

Holloway then got a chance to talk to the waiter, Leclerc, who was couple of years younger than him. He didn't seem cut out for the job as the waiter and attendant for first class on the Paris to Moscow Express. The waiter's temperament had seemed to be one of constant looming dread. His face hung causing a frown, as if he had a massive weight attached to his chin. That seemed to have gone since Holloway and the others stepped back on the train. Leclerc seemed much more relaxed now. Holloway found out more about Leclerc's backstory.

"You have been very helpful to us Leclerc," said Holloway in a grateful fashion.

"Thank you so much sir, but I knew that the train manager was going to kill Mr Travsky. I couldn't tell you though." The young waiter sat down with his head in hands and his face going red.

"What happened?" asked a concerned Holloway.

"My mother needed some treatment for a rare disease, so I stole televisions from a store in Liège to pay for it when I was 15. I was convicted for it. When I joined Russian Railways I lied about my conviction. Colonel Gerasimov knew I lied and threatened to expose me if I didn't keep his secret. But I had to help my family." The waiter looked up in the sky and made a cross.

Holloway put his hand on the waiter's shoulder. At the end of the day, the waiter was a man who cared most for his family. He was willing to pay a high price for his family, but the cost of losing his mother would have been bigger for him. Leclerc's story made Holloway think that there was something about Tatiana's statement that mattered. Would Nikolai reveal himself sometime?

After Nikolai and Alexandra returned to the dining carriage, there was a surprise visitor. This visitor was a shock to Holloway – and everybody else. Dr Goodfortune Joseph had come out of his hermit existence to make amends with Nikolai. The face Nikolai made when Dr Joseph walked into the coach was a face someone would make when chewing excrement. The omens were not good.

"Mr Travsky," said Dr Joseph with his arms outstretched like an Evangelical preacher, "shall we talk?"

"If we must," grunted Nikolai in response as Dr Joseph sat down opposite the oligarch at a table.

"We must have hope, forgiveness and solidarity."

"Don't remind me of those words. How you thought you could grow a business through 'feeling good' is beyond me."

"You need mental well-being and strong teamwork. You need to be at your best."

"No, I need to have a few quiet hours at a desk and low interest rates."

"You see Mr Travsky, your methods are outdated for the challenges of the 21st century."

"In the 21st century, my African division went bust because of your practices."

A shaken Dr Joseph sat down at a Nikolai Travsky's table together and started talking.

"So, Mr Travsky, I am very sorry about what happened to your business in Africa," said Dr Joseph

"Indeed, you should. It was your fault after all."

"Will you apologise for your slandering about me?"

Nikolai looked blankly at Dr Joseph for a moment and said, "since you work for UNESCO, which means that you don't actually do anything to anyone anymore, then I suppose it wouldn't be too costly for me to say sorry."

They shook hands. Dr Stirlitz watched through the door. He and Holloway exchanged nods.

The train trundled into Moscow's Belorussky Station an hour late. Everyone had to show their health certificate to the police on the platform and their temperature was taken. Since it was January, the station was getting dark already despite only being two o' clock in the afternoon. The weather was the vicious combination of frozen air and torrential rain. Not cold enough for decorative snow, too cold for it to be a pleasurable experience to spend a minute outside. The condensation could be seen clearly in the air from passengers and everyone had their warm coats on – except Edmund who was shivering in his trench coat and scarf. Nikolai stepped off the train expecting there to be several dozen people waiting and clapping for him. His wife used her smartphone to record a Facebook live video. A reporter from Russian state news wearing a black puffer jacket with the hood up, along with his cameraman, came up to Nikolai with his blue microphone with 'Rossiya' written on it in white. The journalist shoved the microphone just underneath Nikolai's chin, almost touching it as if he was going to shoot the oligarch with it.

"Mr Travsky," the journalist asked whilst talking very quickly, "Pavel Karamzin from *Rossiya 24* here, what are you doing in Russia? What do you hope to achieve here?"

After a brief rumination, Nikolai said slowly, "to come home and be free."

"Will you be meeting anyone during your stay?"

"This is not a 'stay,' this is a homecoming."

Karamzin thought for a second what to say to Nikolai so he stuck to a familiar line of questioning, "Mr Travsky some people say that you are planning a return to politics here."

"That was not my intention. I was thinking of doing something more enjoyable than going into politics."

Karamzin was puzzled. He enquired, "what is your plan then?"

"To live a simpler and freer life, in prison."

Karamzin gasped and said, "ladies and gentlemen, the news today is that Nikolai Travsky wants to go to jail."

Travsky walked off to a car waiting for him from the hotel. No police had arrested him yet. He did recall the Colonel at Brest taking a call from Moscow. The outcome of the call seemed to be that a higher figure in Moscow wanted to keep him out of danger. Nikolai did not exactly know who this official was and why they were doing it. All he knew was that he was going to the Metropole Hotel for a few days then back home to Paris, not prison. His mission had failed.

Dr Stirlitz, with a fedora in his hand, approached Holloway and

Edmund at the platform.

"Well done," said the German in broken English."

"Thank you very much. I am really sorry about what happened yesterday," replied Holloway.

Stirlitz remarked wryly, "I suppose our interests with Colonel Gerasimov aligned for once," before walking off and disappearing into the dozens of other travellers at the station wearing a long leather jacket.

Holloway seemed taken aback by Stirlitz's statement.

"What do you think of this Edmund?" asked a pensive Holloway, "Stirlitz knew all about Colonel Gerasimov and what he was up to. What is more puzzling is that he suggested he wanted Gerasimov dead."

"Perhaps they are fellow spies who don't get on?" replied the actor.

"He is *definitely* a spy. Who for? The fact that he said our interests don't usually align suggests it is a Russian agency. Probably a rival to the GRU. My guess would be the SVR, the Russian equivalent of MI6."

Holloway and Edmund walked through the concourse of the Belorussky Station. It stank of tobacco – even more so than Paris. The two of them went down an escalator with marble walls and golden chandeliers to the metro. The escalator was so steep that you had to have good balance not to cartwheel forwards down into the abyss. When Holloway and Edmund reached the metro station, the next train was due in about five minutes. There wasn't a crowd on the platform. Just an orderly scattering of metro passengers preparing to board the train. On the walls of the metro station were Socialist Realist mosaics of happy industrious factory workers and a bucolic scene on a collective farm full of tractors. The Moscow metro station just didn't feel right. When Holloway and Edmund eventually got on the train, it wasn't even half full. Maybe, the mosaics were quite appropriate. The factory workers were working long hours and had poor homes to go to. The same could be said for those who toiled on the collective farms. And how were those collective farms conceived? Through the plunder, murdering and deportation of the *Kulaks* in the 1920s and 30s. The scenes of happiness and productivity were really scenes of death and deprivation. No amount of marble bling in Moscow could mask the fact that it was really dying on the inside. The same could be said about London and Paris. A few stops later, Holloway and Edmund stepped off the train into yet another extravagant metro station, this time with mosaics of hydroelectric dams and biplanes and with a slogan above the technological marvels talking about the happiness of mankind.

They emerged out of the subway station into a very non-descript park surrounded by Khrushchev era blocks of flats. The architecture of parts of the city of Coventry was more inspiring. The colour of the concrete blended in very well with the dark grey skies. There was a quite hipsterish hot drinks kiosk, very similar to the one near Edmund's house in Bloomsbury, with warm vintage lighting parked up on one end of the park – the type of fairy lights one might see in a 21st century university student's dingy bedroom. A couple of students were buying drinks from it. Holloway went up to the kiosk to buy Edmund a drink. The thespian sat down on a bench looking towards a play area in the middle of the park. Just one infant watched by her parents was playing on it. Holloway came back to his friend with a plastic drinks cup.

"Americano with almond milk," said Holloway with a grin whilst pointing at Edmund.

"You remembered!" responded Edmund, who grasped the coffee with the hand of his healthy arm, "although I would prefer it in a reusable cup," he said sardonically after staring at the finer details of the cup for a few seconds.

Holloway chuckled and then started to ask Edmund a few questions.

"So," said Holloway with a large exhalation, "what do you think then?"

"The coffee tastes very nice. The beans have clearly been roasted well since you get that wonderful bitterness in the back of your throat. Glad to see they aren't philistines who use Nescafé instant. The almond milk isn't as good as it is in London though."

"Sorry, I meant the journey. Actually, how about the last few months?"

Edmund chuckled, rolled his eyes and blurted out the word "well!"

"Well, what?"

"I have learnt a lot about life. A lot of my previous preconceptions were proven wrong."

Holloway looked a bit startled and probed, "like what?"

"As you know, I have had a fractious rapport with the police forces and security forces in the past."

"Were you a bit of an ACAB?"

"A bit?" laughed Edmund, "no way was I a *bit* of an ACAB. I was a proper ACAB!"

"And what about now?"

"Well, Tidworth probably falls into the bad cop category. He is a total dinosaur and the police force would be better without him. It must be said that without him I would have been poisoned with a nerve agent. Fundamentally, his intentions are in the right place."

"I know I am not a policeman and not as much as a dinosaur as he is..."

"Well, almost," interrupted Edmund with an expression that suggested he demanded precision.

Holloway continued, "I imagine that you wanted to stop the cuts except in the military where you wanted to see a few more."

"Did you just quote Corbyn?" asked a surprised Edmund.

"Yes I did..." replied an aggravated Holloway.

"The point is Captain Holloway or Daniel or Dan, I got it we wrong, we all did during that summer of 2020," the actor paused, "we are all, you know, caught up in the atmosphere and thrill of the events. That euphoria that something could change was undeniably great. Whether that change was going to be any good, that's a different question altogether."

Holloway's body shot back as if he had been electrocuted. "You said what? You said we need the police and military 'more than ever.' Please explain. I am fascinated."

"If the police could have caught Colonel Gerasimov at the beginning, we wouldn't have had to essentially become vigilantes. There seems to be a process. You deplete the security forces, so people have to do it themselves. I could not do what I did today again. Imagine if myself and others in Britain had to take up the role of the police. There would be shootings and stabbings everywhere. We would become like America. How many innocent children would die all because of some sort of dream world that people like myself came up with in the heat of anger and justice?"

Holloway nodded along in pleasure, "now, a devil's advocate might say that today we won."

Edmund pointed to his arm and responded, "we nearly didn't."

"There are some things that Cambridge can't teach! The basics of security seems to be one of them."

"If only I'd have stayed on for another year."

"Don't worry, it wouldn't have helped. In fact, you would have come out worse."

Holloway and Edmund got up after finishing their drinks and headed out of the park towards a road – which was not visible thanks to the traffic jam. By then, it was starting to get dark and one could see the rain lashing down in the car headlights. One car, a black unmarked Mercedes saloon, appear to pull up on the pavement near Edmund and Holloway. It drove off after about ten seconds.

"What was that all about?" asked Edmund.

"Don't worry about it, let's head to Nikolai's hotel!" said a blasé Holloway.

The pair walked off into the torrential rain of the bleak Muscovite rush hour.

News was reaching the higher echelons of Russian intelligence about Nikolai Travsky's arrival in Moscow. The Director of the Western European Department of the SVR, Russia's foreign intelligence agency, Anatoly Isayev, received reports in his oak panelled office about the dissident's presence in Moscow from his secretary. The grey-haired director with browline glasses had a Turkish cigar in his left hand and a Schnapps in his right, which he had developed a taste for whilst posted to the Soviet Embassy in Berlin. He listened to the report whilst slouched on his black leather armchair.

"Director Isayev, Nikolai Travsky was seen arriving at the Belorussky station on the Paris train this afternoon," he said.

Isayev puffed on his cigar, making his secretary cough, before making a large belly laugh with his flabby stomach oscillating, "brilliant, I would like to speak to my old friend."

"Colonel Gerasimov of the GRU was not seen at the station."

The senior spy shook his head witheringly, "they are not what they used to be. Remember how they used to say they were so much better than us? Haven't they realised that people worth hundreds of millions of dollars are much better alive than dead? Who will pay for their adventures? And why was Gerasimov absent?"

"We don't know yet. We know that the man matching his description crossed the border at Brest last night but he has not been seen in Moscow."

"Could he have got off in Minsk?"

"Why would he do that?"

"Well, that is a good question. Why *would* he?" replied the deadpan Spy, "maybe, something happened to Gerasimov on the train meaning that he ended up leaving it early."

"The only possible reason could be his death. Interestingly, the border data from Brest and the CCTV from Belorussky station shows that Captain Daniel Holloway of the British Army's Intelligence Corps was on the train with Nikolai Travsky. He was involved in the death of Sokolova in London back in October. He knew what he was looking for and got rid of Gerasimov."

"That is a very good hypothesis. That is very beneficial for us. It looks like he got the information he needed from the passenger. By the way, does Mr Travsky still have his Maybachs?"

"Yes, as far as I know, but not much else."

"How will he cope with having to economise? I shall make a proposition to him. It will be good to speak to him again. Maybe he could buy more Maybachs."

A security guard came to the door of Isayev's office.

"Yes, who is it?" said Isayev curtly.

"Dr Dirk Stirlitz."

Dr Stirlitz strolled into the office, took off his fedora and smiled at Isayev. Isayev smiled back. They had known each other since the late 1980s from East Berlin. Isayev sat at his dark oak desk, his secretary sat beside the director and Stirlitz sat opposite.

"So, what happened?" enquired an excitable Isayev, speaking very quickly. So quickly in fact that the non-native speaker Stirlitz had to lean in to get a clear idea of what the spy actually said.

"Gerasimov is dead and Nikolai Travsky is back in Russia," replied Stirlitz.

"Excellent, now let's talk to him."

"He is staying at the Hotel Metropol apparently. Room 150."

Isayev picked up the phone and started to call Room 150 at the Metropol. As he was making the call, his assistant turned on the television to show state TV broadcasting the Pavel Karamzin's interview with Nikolai at the station. Isayev slouched back in his chair watching the interview, providing occasional commentary.

"Mr Travsky," he said, "is going to make a very grandiose and vainglorious statement that he won't be able to follow through on."

When Nikolai said that he wanted to go to prison, Isayev laughed and gave a smug look to all his guests as if he understood the temperament of Nikolai Travsky perfectly.

"Nikolai Travsky is *not* going to jail. I have a better way of running him into the ground."

CHAPTER 17: THE MIST AND THE TOWER

About two weeks later, a funeral was held at the Orthodox cemetery in Paris for Alexey Nikolayevich Travsky. Holloway and Tidworth both turned up. Tidworth's white Jaguar sports car was a contrast to the funeral cortège dressed totally in black with the black Mercedes hearse. It seemed a perfect morning for a funeral. Misty, dank, raining and dark. One could just about make out the Eiffel Tower from the elevated position of the cemetery. Tidworth and Holloway dressed in black suits with their black umbrellas up watched the burial from a distance. A group of pall bearers, dressed in black and people who looked about Alexey's age, carried the coffin to its place of rest. A smartly dressed band played Chopin's *Funeral March* – quite ironic that a Polish March was being played at an Orthodox funeral. The band was conducted by Alexey's former music teacher. The wooden coffin was lowered into a hole in the ground. An Orthodox priest in black robes sprayed some incense around the coffin and bellowed out a prayer before the soil was scooped on top of it. Holloway and Tidworth approached Nikolai, who was holding a bag, after the ceremony, and they began talking.

"I hope you are ok today Nikolai," said an apologetic Holloway.
"Condolences Mr Travsky," remarked Tidworth in a very matter of fact manner, to the point of sounding unsympathetic.
"I have reflected more on what you said about my son. I have decided to invite many of his school friends here and his school band. He was a very talented clarinet player." replied Nikolai in

his usually monotonic way – Holloway could see a tiny bit of a thaw though in Nikolai's feelings for his son again. Nikolai then took the conversation in an unexpected direction. "You know how Tatiana said that losing her family was not a big cost, I think she is right. I blame myself – Alexandra blames herself too. I sent her off to boarding school in England. She wanted to see us, but she couldn't. Alexey too. Even though he wasn't at boarding school, we didn't see much of him as well because we were working all the time. We weren't really proper parents looking back. We just let them find their own way. When they both needed our help and support, there was nobody there for them. I have learnt over the last few years what really matters. I am increasingly convinced that a close-knit and caring family is absolutely vital for children, and I am ashamed I did not realise that before. It could have prevented so much pain. By the way, how is your friend, Edmund?"

Holloway responded by saying, "he is fine, thank you. I believe he has been able to rent somewhere else much nicer in London thanks to the 30 thousand you provided us with for security on the train. When I get back to London, I will probably meet up him."

"I am very happy for Edmund. I told you he would be loyal to you. He delivered in the end despite your scepticism. What are *you* going to do with your money?"

"I don't know. Buy a nice car maybe, go on holiday or something like that," replied Holloway and shrugged his shoulders to show that he didn't really know what to say.

"Well, it won't be as nice as mine," Tidworth chipped in.

Turning to Nikolai's political predicament, Holloway asked a rhetorical question, "so, you didn't go to jail then?"

"No, I didn't," replied a visibly bitter Nikolai, clenching his lips.

Holloway sighed in frustration at the oligarch's dubious aims and said, "I think you need to take the positives from it."

"What are the positives? It could have been the revitalisation of my political career."

"So, you are even more of a cynic than I thought! All that stuff about 'freedom' and wanting to escape money was your spiel to myself and the media," Holloway replied whilst rolling his eyes.

"People like a man who says that he wants to sacrifice everything for a cause – like Navalny did in 2021. I know this sounds like a paradox, but my country is both in stagnation and decline. The social contract gradually degrading before our eyes with a leadership that has no interest in reinvigorating it. They would be happy to watch their nation crumble in front of them if it meant keeping their funds. Russia is not just sick, it is suffering from multiple organ failure. Russia doesn't need a rest and some vitamins, it needs fixing, now!"

In the end, Nikolai Travsky did seem to be an empty individual. His quest for political martyrdom, heavily tinged with self-promotion, had failed. Despite feeling remorse about how he neglected his family, he seemed to overlook the views of his wife on his political quest. She would have simply been dragged along to prison and be expected to muddle through. There was something even more troubling about Nikolai's circumstances. There were several chances for the Russian authorities to arrest him: on entry at Brest, his short stay in Moscow and on his exit from the country. So why didn't the authorities follow through on such an obvious task? Holloway thought it unwise to ask explicitly. It was like a crab was nipping his legs with its claws. The questions were nagging the naturally curious intelligence officer who was desperate to find out why Nikolai hadn't gone to prison when there was motive, means and opportunity.

Before probing Nikolai further, Holloway decided to change the subject onto a more amenable topic for Tidworth who had been puffing, tutting and tapping his feet throughout with crossed arms whilst Nikolai delivered his monotonic political *denouement*.

"I found this case an interesting opportunity to cooperate with the police for the first time," said Holloway.

"You did ok," replied Tidworth with a shrug of the shoulders which turned to a grin where one could see his rather yellow teeth with rather uneven gaps between them.

"He nearly took a bullet for me," said Nikolai, who still managed to sound antipathetic when thanking someone for saving his life.

"Thanks, I know it hasn't gone smoothly with you, really appreciate that," replied Holloway.

"I am interested to know, from a security point of view, what do you think was the most crucial variable in solving this case?" asked Nikolai.

"Borders," answered Tidworth, "I preferred it when countries were countries and you knew where they were. You have to have strong border screening. Our border screening was not strong enough, so Gerasimov left the UK unnoticed. We could have nabbed him. We are a load of wet wipes on this issue in the UK – and we always pay for it."

"People underestimate for us in security how easy it is for criminals to slip through when you don't know who is coming in and out of your country. The pandemic proved that we needed to know who was coming into the country. Biosecurity is national security. Who would have even known that Gerasimov was in Paris without him being checked at the airport on camera?" argued Holloway.

"Do you think he was naive?" asked Nikolai.

"Certainly not. I think he thought he would be able to get away with it all because he had such success before. As I believe I said on the train, arrogance was his downfall. This isn't like the 'good old days' of Schengen. We thought that history would end with there being no borders, no differences, no nations even. They were all just "imagined communities" and "invented traditions" that would eventually become obsolete. Well look how good our international organisations were when we needed them the most!"

Tidworth looked a little bit left out of yet another very philosophical discussion. He had a very bemused face. His mouth was slightly open as if he was about to say something whilst showing absolutely no attempt to join in the conversation - until the question of alcoholic drinks came around.

"What should we do the toast with?" Tidworth asked.

"Ah, yes the most important question of them all. I have a fine bottle of Vodka in this bag from somebody. We shall share it out!" exclaimed Nikolai.

"Bit kitsch isn't it?" said Holloway.

"I don't have enough feelings to be ashamed!"

The three toasted to the memory of Alexey. The mist started to lift so that you could see the Eiffel Tower a bit clearer.

After the toast, the three went into a nearby brasserie. The lighting was subdued, there were spartan wooden tables and chairs and the walls were dotted with posters advertising shows in Montmartre from the 1890s. The oligarch leant over to Holloway and told him to go with him to a corner of the restaurant. He was nervous that others might overhear what was being said.

"One thing I have not told you yet, since I don't think I have found the appropriate moment. But this is very important," said Nikolai so quickly that Holloway had to ask him to repeat, "I had a visit from an 'old friend' whilst I was in Moscow. A man in a very significant position within the security services - the SVR to be exact. He told me that there was a plot to kidnap me by factions in the security services whilst I was in Moscow and, thanks to his intervention, he stopped it from happening. In return, he would like me to consider returning to Russia."

"Don't listen to him, he sounds like a total fantasist! To what end? What would be the point of that? The fact that, thanks to his intervention, he stopped a plot to kidnap shows it isn't safe anyway," replied Holloway.

"What I said is not the full *quid pro quo*?"

"What is he offering you? Freedom from arrest?"

"Protection, for now, from arrest and persecution. The senior official, and I think he is right, believes that my country needs to take a different path. There is evidence that there could be a shuffle at the top of the current leadership in the spring. If I return to Russia in March, permanently, I would be offered a senior job in the revitalised administration."

"So what? What if there is no revitalised administration?"

"There is more. He offered to reinstate all of my frozen assets from 2012. I could be a lot richer again."

"And how long will the protection from arrest and persecution last?"

"That was only this trip, to prevent me from becoming an opposition martyr. My liberty was in both of our interests then. From March, anything could happen."

"Do you choose your vanity or your security?"

The mist dropped over the Eiffel Tower again.

AFTERWORD

The most evocative quote I have ever heard about endings is that of Dr Seuss: "don't cry because it's over, smile because it happened." I do hope that you are smiling and that if you are crying, you are having tears of joy, not anguish.

If you hated this story, it is mercifully short. If you really liked the past few pages, you are in luck because there is a sequel in the pipeline. Captain Daniel Holloway, DCI Len Tidworth and Nikolai and Alexandra Travsky will return in:

BLACK SQUARE

ABOUT THE AUTHOR

James Meakin

James Meakin has an Upper-Second Class degree in History from Durham University and will be starting an MA in History from the same institution in the autumn of 2021. He specialises in the political and cultural history of late Third Republic France. James has further interests in Restoration-era England, modern Russian history and general military history.

The author developed an enthusiasm for military affairs from being the son of a former officer in the Royal Corps of Transport (now Royal Logistics Corps) who served in Cyprus, West Germany and Northern Ireland and had a stint attached to the Intelligence Corps.

Outside of writing and his studies, James is an avid cricket fan, learning French and Russian and is an occasional pianist. He keeps a blog where he writes about Russian and Belarusian affairs.

Printed in Great Britain
by Amazon

63501388R00104